MUSTANG FEVER

MUSTANG FEVER

GARY McCARTHY

DOUBLEDAY & COMPANY, INC.

GARDEN CITY, NEW YORK

1980

All the characters in this book are fictitious, and any resemblance to actual persons, living or dead, is purely coincidental.

Library of Congress Cataloging in Publication Data

McCarthy, Gary.
  Mustang fever.

  1. Mustang—Legends and stories. I. Title.
PZ4.M12293Mu [PS3563.A25915]   813'.5'4

        ISBN: 0-385-15472-0
Library of Congress Catalog Card Number 79-7501

*To my brother
Dr. Ken McCarthy
and to our riding days*

MUSTANG FEVER

CHAPTER 1

When Darby Buckingham saw the mustangs, his face went pale with cold fury and he actually bit his Cuban cigar in half.

A moment before, he had been the picture of contentment, with his chair tipped back precariously against the front of the Antelope Hotel. Because of his enormous size and manner of dress, he was a striking figure, particularly in the Wyoming cattle town of Running Springs. He was an Easterner, a renowned dime novelist and proud of it. From his round-toed black shoes to his round, black derby hat, he presented the exact appearance of a man of considerable taste and wealth; Darby Buckingham had both, and more.

The front legs of his chair crashed down on the boardwalk so forcefully that he even startled Miss Dolly Beavers. No mean feat. Once she warmed to a topic, there was little or nothing a man could do or say to divert her attention. But the look on Darby's face, and the way his cigar popped out of his teeth, bitten clean off, stopped her cold.

"What is it, darling?"

"Have you ever seen anything like that, Dolly?"

Her sharp intake of breath answered his question. The mustangs were being driven up Main Street by a crew of men. As they passed by building after building, Darby saw the town's merchants appear at their doors, faces reflecting shock, then anger and disgust.

"Good God!" Dolly cried. "What have they done to those horses?"

Darby rose to his feet, a hard knot forming in his throat. "They've wired their nostrils shut so they can't *breathe* well enough to run. They've put sacks over their eyes so they can't *see* well enough to run." His big fists balled at his sides. "But still, they must have tried. So they shackled their legs with a length of chain and let them run until they beat themselves bloody."

Dolly's hand flew to her mouth. "They look horrible," she moaned. "Darby, can't you do something?"

"I can try," he said. "But there's no law that I know of against cruelty to horses." There should be, he thought, watching the animals approach.

Darby Buckingham wasn't a tall man, but he possessed a depth of chest and shoulders that represented a challenge for the best of tailors. His neck seemed more like an extension of his shoulders and the collar he wore was as big around as a woman's waist. Those who knew him swore his neck sank into those massive shoulders when he grew angry and his thick, battered hands clenched into fighter's fists.

At such moments, there wasn't a sensible man alive who would have believed that the mild, urbane, overweight eastern dude they'd seen only seconds before could have been transformed into the awesome block of man they now beheld. But a bulldog, asleep or at play, is not the same animal that it becomes in combat. Not the same at all.

Darby was on his feet and his eyes studied the procession. The mustangs were piteous. They were thin to the point of being emaciated. Their heads hung nearly to their knees and their mouths were open, gasping into the small clouds of dust that their hoofs created. Blindfolded, they shuffled like walking dead and Darby Buckingham had the fleeting impression that no defeated army was ever taken from their land in a more wretched state.

There were about fifty head and they were tightly bunched, coughing dust, stepping blindly into one another. They must have realized they were entering the world of man, but Darby saw no sign of fear, nor of resistance. They looked and acted as if they'd been driven through hell and wanted only to lie down and die. Though Darby did not have a great fondness for horses, and was aware of the harshness of the West, this seemed too much for a civilized man to swallow. He stepped off the boardwalk and into the street.

"Hey! Get the hell out of the way!" a man yelled, urging his horse forward.

Darby's neck sunk deeper into his shoulders, his thick black mustache bristled. He was not a man to initiate a fight and found no need to prove himself; he'd done that too many times in a prize ring during his youth. Besides, his strength was of such renown, it pained him to exercise it against most men. But this was different.

As the mustangs grew nearer, he winced with something akin to real personal pain as he saw the disfiguring wires stitched through their noses. There wasn't an animal in the herd that wasn't limping. The chain was attached to one leg only and it wasn't long. Two feet at most. Just enough, he thought, to crack their hocks and pasterns if they traveled faster than a trot. He snorted with disgust. Not one among them looked to have the strength or spirit left to escape a running child.

"Out of the way, I said! Stupid dude. You want to get trampled?"

Darby forced his eyes from the mustangs and stood rooted in the street. He watched a big man with a strong, brutal face spur forward.

"Can't you hear?" The cowboy swore, sliding his mount to a standstill only a few feet from where Darby stood.

"I can hear," Darby replied. "Are you the man responsible for that?"

"What?" The cowboy's face was hard, his eyes piercing. He started to reach for a quirt that dangled from his saddle horn, but Darby tensed to strike and he pulled his hand away. He glanced up at Dolly Beavers and something almost resembling a smile split his thin lips.

"Ma'am, if this . . . fellar is a friend of yours, you'd sure better come down and lead him out of the street. Me and the boys are at the end of a long day and not much of a mind to cater to an idiot."

The herd was almost on them. "My name is Paxton Bullock and we'll be needing rooms and corrals for these horses. We can pay your price. We work for Hench Hightower in Nevada. Now for the last time, ma'am, would you tell him to git!"

Darby took three quick steps forward, and before Paxton could rein his horse into his path, Darby grabbed the cowboy by the cartridge belt and leg. Paxton's eyes widened in disbelief and he clawed for his gun. But it was too late. The ramrod weighed no less than two hundred and twenty pounds, but he came out of his saddle with surprising speed.

"Ahhh!" Darby bellowed, heaving the man bodily.

Paxton was a natural athlete. He hit the ground in a rolling dive and came up bent on his knees with his gun aimed.

Darby Buckingham heard Dolly scream and someone else shout, "Hold it, you're covered!"

Paxton's eyes shifted toward the voice, then seemed to have caught a movement farther down the street. His shoulders slumped and when he returned his gaze to Darby, there was pure hatred in every word he spoke. A rasp, no more, and for Darby alone. "I see an old man with a sheriff's badge and a gun aimed at me from the far corner of the street. Half a block down, there's two more geezers in buckskins lying face down on the sidewalk with buffalo rifles as big as my leg—them rifles are pointed at me too! Now I don't know what the hell has gotten you stirred up, mister, but you've pushed your game to the limit. Back off or . . ."

"Or what?" Darby growled.

"Or we're both going to get ourselves buried, right now!" Paxton's eyes narrowed. He paused for a long moment. "I'm afraid of no man living and if I ever come across your trail in Nevada, you're meat. But right now, I don't see no reason to die in a standoff. So I'm putting up my gun."

Darby hadn't realized it but he'd been holding his breath; he expelled it slowly, but when he saw the mustangs again— those nostrils—he figured nothing had been settled.

Zeb Cather strode out, the badge on his chest glinting in the sun. He was on the high side of sixty, but the gun rested in his hand in a way that left no doubt he could use it. "What the hell is going on?" he asked gruffly.

"Damned if I know," Paxton spat, rising to his feet and slapping dust off himself. "This crazy man wouldn't get off the street and let me and my wranglers pass. I asked him but he seemed to have some burr stuck under his saddle. First thing I know, he's got ahold of me and I'm on the ground."

"Darby?" The sheriff's pale blue eyes shifted to his friend. "Is he tellin' the truth?"

"Of course," Darby replied. "The entire town watched it happen." He saw a look of surprise, then confidence, in Paxton's face.

"Hell," the big ramrod said. "He even admits it! You going to lock him up? You'd better, you know. If he ever lays a hand on me again, I'll kill him in self-defense."

"You do," a voice drawled, "you'll have two holes bigger'n boot tops to see through."

Darby turned, knowing very well who'd spoken. It was Zack Woolsey and right beside him stood the immovable mountain, Bear Timberly. They were buffalo hunters, frontiersmen of bygone days. And when they made a statement, it was as good as their word. He saw Paxton's eyes shift, tighten thoughtfully. Perhaps he hadn't been worried about an eastern dude or even an aging sheriff but he sure wasn't taking Zack or Bear lightly.

Paxton spun his attention back to the sheriff. "I can understand now why a man your age is still carrying a badge in this town."

"Mind your mouth," Zeb warned. "I can carry this badge on my own."

"Can you! Well, all I know is that we rode in here peacea-

ble and ready to drop some money in this two-bit town.
First thing I get is trouble and you're sticking up for the
dude."

Darby Buckingham pointed at the mustangs. "Can he do
that, Zeb?"

"You mean the wires?"

"Yes, the wires and chains and sacking over their eyes.
Those animals are half-dead!"

The sheriff absently dropped his gun into his holster,
scrubbed his jaw thoughtfully. Darby could tell by the way
he was stalling that there was nothing unlawful about Paxton's methods. When Zeb Cather spoke, he sounded apolo-
getic.

"Sorry, Darby. Those are wild horses and property of the
man who catches them. I can't do a thing."

"Hell no, you can't!" Paxton snorted. He jabbed a finger
at Darby. "And if the big fat man here is so damned
worried about 'em, maybe you'll let us pass on to the livery.
We'll feed and water 'em same as our saddle horses."

"Your kindness overwhelms me," Darby said tightly.

Paxton's face went crimson and his body left no doubt he
wanted to swing. Darby hoped he would. "I got a job to do
and I don't give a damn what you or anyone else says. I answer to only one man—Hench Hightower out of Elko, Nevada. We catch these horses and sell 'em any damn place we
can."

"And where have you sold these?" Darby asked.

"To a man in Cheyenne."

"And what will he do with them?"

Paxton sneered. "Who cares? Hides are going for two dollars and tails at four bits. Rest might feed dogs or pigs."

A strong hand grabbed Darby's arm and Zack said,
"You're wrong about this, Darby. It's no different than all
those years Bear and me shot buffalo and sold the hides."

Darby whirled around. "Isn't it!" he demanded, looking
straight into Zack's eyes. "Take a good look at those animals. At least the bison died quickly."

Zack Woolsey's glance dropped into the dirt and Darby, shrugging his arm free, bulled his way toward the Antelope Hotel. He needed a drink.

Darby's room was on the second floor, overlooking Main Street. Since going upstairs, he'd tried to forget about Paxton and the mustangs by piling all his trunks onto the bed and lifting the whole mass again and again until he was nearly exhausted. Normally, such exertion brought on a sense of lassitude and well-being. But not this night. He finally gave up the lifting and spent a few minutes at his desk. It was time to start another dime novel for the New York Publishing House. His editor and friend, J. Franklin Warner, had been more than patient since Darby's arrival in Running Springs. But his most recent letters carried a message of real concern that Buckingham readers were starting to grow impatient.

Darby fiddled with paper and ink, trying to rework several parts of his latest book centering around Zack Woolsey and Bear Timberly. They were real characters, those two, and his story would be a good one. Lucky, Darby thought, that Paxton hadn't pulled back the hammer on his revolver—Bear and Zack would have killed him for sure.

Raucous laughter erupted on the street and Darby, searching for distraction, rose from his desk and peered out the window. The angle was just right and he could see Paxton and his men moving toward the Bull Dog Bar. Darby's mustache crept down at the corners of his mouth in a grimace. Paxton and his buckaroos didn't have a care in the world.

Darby whirled around, then stopped short of the doorway as a knock and the lilting voice of Dolly Beavers froze him.

"Yoo-hoo! Derby honey. I know you're in there so you might as well open up. Remember . . . I have passkeys."

Damn the passkeys! he thought. There was a lot to be said for Dolly. He was actually quite fond of the woman, and her blond hair and voluptuous figure pleased him—but not tonight. He just wasn't in the mood. Neither the lifting nor writing had been able to take his mind off those mustangs, and Dolly Beavers, despite her considerable charms, wouldn't fare differently.

"Dolly, I'm not dressed," he rumbled.

The sound of the passkey in his lock caused him to lift his hands beseechingly toward the ceiling. Was nothing sacred anymore? Didn't the woman understand the word privacy?

Angry, and feeling bested by her as usual, he yanked the door open. Dolly, propelled by her forward momentum, tripped on her skirt and toppled into him. She grabbed him by the waist on her way down and, trying to catch her, they both spilled over backward onto the rug.

"Well, my," she giggled, blowing an errant gold lock from her eyes, "isn't this a pleasant surprise. We've done this before, you know." Devilishly, she tweaked his nose.

"Dolly! Get off of me!"

Her face clouded. "What's the matter?" she asked, genuinely concerned. "Are you still upset about what happened outside?"

"Yes."

"So am I." She sighed, then laid her head on his chest. "It's terrible what they did. But you heard the sheriff, Derby. They haven't broken the law."

"Hang the law!" he snapped. "Dolly, would you mind if we carried on this conversation upright? The door is standing wide open."

"Then kick it shut, silly. Your legs *are* short, dear, but not that short."

"Get off," he ordered.

Reluctantly, she complied.

After rearranging his suit, Darby began to pace back and forth, trying to sort out his thoughts by talking.

"I've thought it over and I can't, in all conscience, allow that to happen," he began. "Zack was wrong comparing a horse to a bison. A horse is a thing of some intelligence and beauty. To be torn from its range, driven blind and gasping like that only to be shot for hide and hair, is revolting. And if there is no law against it, there ought to be."

"Derby," she said calmly, "I've lived out here all my life and men have always caught wild horses. Most of them roam in Nevada and I've met many cowboys who caught mustang fever and never were worth a hoot for anything afterward."

"Mustang fever?"

"That's what they call it," she said, nodding. "It's no different from . . . say, gold fever. A mustanger's eyes will light up when he starts to talking about the chase. There's' nothing you can do to change that."

"I don't want to change that!" he cried. "Believe me, I can appreciate what the excitement must be racing down on a herd of wild horses. It must require skill and courage of the highest order. But what I do not accept is the outcome. Is that all they're worth, Dolly? A trifling two dollars and fifty cents for their skin?"

"Hide," she corrected. "No, usually they are sold for saddle horses. The Army buys a great many and ranchers, miners, and cowboys most of the rest. Some of the larger ones wind up pulling a plow or wagon."

"Even that's not so bad," Darby said, morosely.

She came to stand before him. Her perfume was too strong, as usual, but he knew she loved him and that offset most everything. "Derby, please cheer up. There's nothing you can do about those mustangs. I haven't heard about that sort of cruelty in years and I'd thought wiring nostrils was no longer used. But, apparently, this Hench Hightower lets his crews do it and that's something you or I can't change. Now," she said softly, "is there something I can do to help take your mind off those poor mustangs?"

He kissed her softly. "No," he said. "I'm afraid not, Dolly. I guess I ought to take a walk on the prairie and I'd prefer it alone."

"I understand."

Darby watched her leave and shook his head in appreci-

ation. The best part of her was that she really did understand.

The stars glittered, silver specks against an indigo ex-
panse. The writer's eyes lifted toward the pale outline of the
Tetons, still crested with snow so white it seemed almost to
glow. Far to the west, he heard a coyote howl and a mild
breeze filled the air with the tangy scent of mesquite. Often
he walked the prairie just after dark, sometimes alone, fre-
quently with Dolly Beavers. There was a quiet stillness, a
forever sense of vastness that profoundly moved him and
filled him with peace. But not tonight.

He turned away from the mountains, and his eyes carried
back to Running Springs and then rested on the lone lamplight he knew would be the livery.

Darby lit a cigar. He had a decision to make. He could
walk back to the Antelope Hotel and go to bed and in the
morning Paxton and his crew would be gone . . . or . . . he
could take a stand against cruelty and run the danger of getting shot for his interference. The Cuban cigar glowed
brightly as he puffed ever faster, then started toward
the livery. He was a fool, he told himself, walking rapidly.
And Dolly was right because, no matter how he acted now,
Hench Hightower's crews would go right on catching mustangs for the same purpose. Nothing he could do to stop
that. Maybe. But it might be worth trying—and there might
be one hell of a good story down in the Nevada mustang
country.

As he neared the livery, he began to whistle a soft tune.
The decision made, he felt better. With any luck, Paxton
and most of his crew would go on drinking for a few more
hours. More than enough time to do what he intended. Afterward, he'd take the consequences whatever they might
be. He wasn't carrying a gun, which might save his life if he
ran into Paxton. As far as Darby was concerned, a six-
shooter was worthless. He'd tried to learn how to use one.
Sheriff Cather had spent hours discussing the finer points of
how to draw, cock back the hammer, and fire accurately.

But it was wasted time and effort. Darby's fingers were thick and short and totally incapable of handling anything much more complex than a quill pen. When he'd shot through his own holster twice attempting the fast draw, even Zeb Cather gave up. They agreed right on the spot that since he couldn't draw and he never hit what he fired at, Darby should avoid the holstered gun entirely. They'd settled on a derringer and a shotgun as Darby's only two alternatives should trouble ever force him into gunplay. But as he skirted the livery and headed for the corral, he was unarmed and hoping he hadn't made a fatal mistake. One thing was certain, he'd seen a murderous intent in Paxton Bullock's eyes. If it hadn't been for the sheriff, Zack, and Bear, the Hightower ramrod would have pulled the trigger right on Main Street.

Darby walked up to the corral and peered through the bars. He wasn't eager to go inside but there was no other way.

"Evenin', mister."

Darby, one leg half-raised to step through the pole, froze. His back muscles stiffened with fear and he slowly pulled his leg back and turned toward the voice. He was halfway expecting a bullet.

"What do you have in mind? Trouble, I bet."

Darby squinted, searching for the voice. He located it in the semidarkness. A boy. Not really, he thought, walking closer, but he wasn't a man yet either. What Darby did notice with obvious relief was that the kid wasn't holding a gun. In fact, he wasn't even wearing one.

"My name is Darby Buckingham," he said, stopping when he was near enough to see the kid's face clearly.

"Yeah." There was no show of curiosity, no change of expression on the young, smooth face. Just a patient waiting for a question unanswered.

"I want to buy those mustangs. Now."

"Huh." The impassive face amazingly produced a half

smile. "What for?" he asked. "I don't think you could ride a one of 'em."

"What is your name?"

"Jory Parnes. Why do you want to buy 'em?"

"Does it matter to you?" Darby asked quietly.

Jory thought it over carefully. "Nope," he said after a long pause. "I guess it don't."

Darby felt a touch of disappointment toward the kid. He was working for the right outfit.

"No matter what you need 'em for, Mr. Buckingham, they'll be better off. If you wanted to turn 'em loose in the morning, then shoot 'em for target practice, they'd still be better off."

"I see." Darby's thick, black eyebrows furrowed thoughtfully. He wondered how much to tell the boy. One thing for sure, he needed his help. "Jory, how much for the lot? Name a price with which your boss will be happy. I don't want you getting into trouble."

"Price is easy. Two fifty each, forty-eight horses." Jory shook his head and shrugged apologetically. "I ain't much at numbers."

"Nor am I. Let's make it easy for both of us. Fifty head would make it one hundred and twenty-five dollars. Fair enough?"

"Mister," Jory said, sticking out his hand, "I don't know what you've got in mind, but it's a deal."

"Good," Darby sighed.

"You can come back first thing in the morning. Paxton will be happy not to have to go on to Cheyenne. Besides, along the way a few would have died."

Darby nodded. "One problem, Jory. I want them now. It's between you and me."

"Huh," Jory grunted. "I can understand why you don't want to meet the boss after what happened before, but I can't figure out the horses at all."

Darby laughed. "You will soon enough, young man. I just hope Mr. Bullock is as satisfied as you think he's going to be. Let's get to work."

CHAPTER 2

Darby Buckingham emerged from the livery barn with two pairs of hoof nippers. He handed one pair to Jory Parnes. "You know what we're going to do," he said.

For a second, Jory hesitated as though unsure. Then he took the nippers and grinned with satisfaction. "I sure do."

The job went fast. One by one, they cut out the hated nostril wires. And though the mustangs were fearful and shuddered when touched, Darby thought they must have understood. Jory kept up a steady, soothing line of talking to them. Darby tried it too, although he couldn't think of much to say. He finally decided to recite some Shakespeare and expound on the delicacies of fish and fowl poached with French white wines. And as he talked, every snip of the wire brought him a huge sense of satisfaction. The only drawback, he discovered, was that the conversation made him hungry. Despite this, they worked quickly and were finished in less than an hour.

The leg chains were a bit more challenging. They were attached to a single leather hobble on the left foreleg, right over the hock. The trick was to unbuckle the strap. But the horses were very touchy about their feet and lower legs. Probably, Darby realized, it stemmed from a natural fear of becoming entangled or even snake-bit. But the two men soon had a routine worked out. Since the mustangs were still blindfolded with the sacking, Darby would wrap an arm around their necks and hold them steady while Jory's quick fingers loosened the straps. The writer's strength and weight served them well and he couldn't help thinking they made a damn good team.

As they raced to finish before Paxton returned, Darby felt better than he had in a long time. His suit, always spotless, became coated with horsehair and sweat. More than one mustang reared or spun him flying into the dirt. He didn't care. He was having too much fun. Darby guessed that the kid was enjoying himself in the same way; it was obvious Jory's enthusiasm went far beyond doing a job. Several times, Darby found himself marveling at the speed and agility of the young cowboy. He seemed to have a soothing yet efficient way of handling horses that Darby hadn't seen before, even among the wranglers who frequented this part of Wyoming. They unstrapped the last chain and grinned at each other with approval.

He stepped back from the corral, puffing for breath, but feeling real exhilaration as he watched the herd begin to circle and show life. With their chains off and nostrils reopened, the mustangs were transformed. Snorting and prancing, they tossed their covered heads and bugled with restiveness. These were the mustangs he soon hoped to see! Darby itched to tear the sacking from their eyes and witness them as they were meant to be. But how? The way they were charging around the corral made it seem impossible.

"Mr. Buckingham," Jory said, "I think you'd better let me handle the rest."

Darby didn't argue. He wasn't the horseman—that was Jory Parnes' role. But he'd carried his share of the job so far and was reluctant to sit back now. "It could be very exciting in there," he offered.

"Yeah, it could be," Jory said evenly. "Make no mistake, those mustangs are wild and they'll go after a man once they can see him."

"Then we'll have to ride in?"

"Can you ride?"

Darby started to say yes, but stopped. What was accurate was that he could stay in the saddle well enough to go from one location to another when necessary. But in Jory's world, that probably wouldn't be considered riding.

"That's what I thought," Jory said. "You climb up on the top rail and hang on tight. This won't take long."

Before Darby could reply, the kid was striding into the darkness to find his horse. Darby grinned down at the mustangs and took a deep, satisfied breath. Sitting on the rail, he'd soon witness their return to the world of sight. Maybe they would show their appreciation by trying to stomp their liberators into the ground. Maybe they had the right.

I wonder, he thought, which one is the stallion? He reminded himself to ask Jory before they set them all free. He'd heard a lot of stories about wild stallions. About how they'd impale themselves trying to leap a pole corral, and even about one who hurled himself off a cliff rather than submit to man. In the West, there were stallions as famous as gunslingers. Crafty, treacherous when trapped, willing to fight and die for the sake of escape, such horses became admired and chased by every man with a rope and a dream of owning what could never be truly owned. To Darby Buckingham, and he was sure his eastern readers would agree, the wild stallion epitomized the indomitable spirit of freedom.

He studied each animal carefully. Which one was it? Even if this stallion wasn't so wise and had allowed himself to get caught, Darby had a hunch he'd be easy enough to spot by the fierce, challenging look in his eye. When the hated sacking was finally lifted, it would be thrilling to see him lead his band out through the open gate to freedom. It would be a sight he guessed he'd probably remember all his life.

"Jory," he called, "which one is the stallion?"

Even in the poor lamplight from the livery, Darby saw the kid stiffen in his saddle. Then, as though he hadn't heard the question, Jory reached down from his horse and started to unlatch the gate.

"Jory," Darby called again. "Point out the stallion."

The young man straightened up in his saddle. He shook his head sadly. "The stallion is dead, Mr. Buckingham.

Hench Hightower makes it his policy to shoot every one of
'em first chance."

"But . . . but, why! Why, damnit!"

Jory yanked the gate open. "It's because they'll always be
dangerous. They'll do anything for freedom and even when
they lose their band, they'll raid a rancher's herd for mares
and start another. Mr. Hightower don't like that, he says a
stallion costs him money."

Darby squeezed the top rail until his knuckles turned
white. "Be careful," he gritted.

Jory wasn't careful. He spurred his mount into the herd
and Darby saw the flash of a knife blade again and again as
he slit the leather thongs that tied the sacking just under the
throat. Jory didn't waste time even to pull the mask free, but
spurred after another horse. Darby watched him with fasci-
nation. The herd became a swirling melee and the mustangs
began to strike at the pole corral, at each other, and at Jory
Parnes. A cloud of dust rose, became choking. Darby's eyes
stung and he pulled a handkerchief from his pocket and
pressed it over his face to breathe through. But he wouldn't
have moved or taken his eyes off the rider for anything. In
and out, half-seated, half-leaning one way then the next,
Jory worked both horse and knife like extensions of his lithe
body. His horse needed no reining but darted and dodged
after its quarry with what Darby suspected was only the
slightest touch of leg pressure and a perfect union with his
master. In five minutes, it was all over.

Darby leapt from the rail and swung the gate open. And
then . . . the mustangs were running for the high Tetons
with their tails flying. They vanished into the night, but he
listened to the sound of their hoofbeats for a long time. He
would have given anything to see their stallion leading them
to freedom, but even without that, he stood in the dust and
smiled contentedly.

Afterward, he took Jory aside. He was probably wasting
his breath, but Darby knew he had to try. "Jory," he began

hesitantly. "I have the feeling you enjoyed setting them loose."

The kid shoved his hat back and the top of his exposed forehead looked egg-white to the hairline. He grinned. "Yeah, Mr. Buckingham, I liked it plenty."

"Good. What will happen to those mustangs without a stallion?"

"Oh, they'll be back on their home range long before we will, I reckon. And some big stud will find 'em even before that."

"I hope the next one is a little smarter," Darby said.

"Oh, the last one was no fool. He just wasn't quite fast enough to outrun Paxton's rifle slug."

"I see." Darby frowned. "Does it have to be that way?"

"I don't think so."

"Neither do I," Darby rumbled. "How would you like to help me change things?"

Jory's head jerked up. "What do you mean?" he asked quickly.

"I'm not sure," Darby admitted. "But I'd like to see if something can be done about this Mr. Hench Hightower."

Jory laughed with a harsh, brittle sound. "You don't know what you'd be letting yourself in for. He wouldn't allow it."

"He has no choice," Darby retorted hotly. "If he's working on government land, those horses belong to anyone who is smarter or tougher."

Jory's glance dropped to his boots and he edged a round circle of dirt. "Sure," he whispered.

Darby lit up a cigar, making a great pretense of lighting it properly. The writer knew that Jory Parnes was thinking he was a dude and an eccentric from back East with too much money and too little sense. Well, Darby thought, maybe that was mostly true. But since arriving in Running Springs, he'd handled more than a little trouble and he was still alive. There was a story in Nevada about mustangs and Darby meant to write it—there was a man named Hightower and he meant to break him—if he could.

"Jory," he said, "I guess I'll turn in for the night. Come by in the morning when the bank opens; I'll have Paxton's money." He started to walk away.

"Mr. Buckingham?"

"Yes?" he asked with sudden hope.

"Good night, sir. And thanks."

"Thank you," Darby replied. "Think about what I said, young man. I am not to be dismissed lightly."

Darby was almost out of hearing when Jory's voice reached him. "I believe that."

Jory Parnes was nineteen, but he'd been doing a man's work since he was old enough to throw a rope and ride the kinks out of the meanest bronc. He wasn't going to be a big man, and it galled him that, even in his boots, he didn't measure six feet. Nor was he particularly strong like Paxton or Darby Buckingham. But he had a lean, tensile toughness and he carried not an ounce of fat. Hard work and early years in the saddle were already beginning to shape his legs into that particular curve of a horseman. Had he been a large man, Jory would have lacked the physique that marked an exceptional rider. His litheness and stature befitted his calling, and men who had watched bronc riders all their lives said Jory Parnes was going to be as good as the best. It was his greatest pride. Breaking wild horses was a deadly business, and after a man got trampled or a horse busted up his legs by hurling itself at a tree or corral, many riders turned against horseflesh. But not Jory. As far as he was concerned, the horse was the finest animal that walked the earth and man was no exception.

He respected, admired, and loved every horse he ever sat and even the outlaws that tried to bury him elicited no change in his attitude. For horses, he knew, weren't naturally vicious. They could be beaten with quirts, spurred bloody with a pair of Mexican rowels, and raced until their hearts burst. They did as they were willed, and if one rebelled, then maybe it was a little wiser than most.

This mustanging, he thought as he unsaddled his horse and turned it back into its pen, was the sorriest business he'd ever gotten himself into. He'd worked for Hench Hightower almost eighteen months and hated every day. Hench kept three crews scouring the mountains east and west of Elko, Nevada. But Paxton was the worst of them all. At first, he'd tried to believe that the big ramrod was just following orders. Later, he knew that Paxton was just plain mean. He could get away with it too, because he was handy with a gun and terrible to watch in a fist fight. More than once, Jory had seen him take a club to a horse and knock it senseless; he'd do the same to any cowboy who crossed his trail. Jory was afraid of Paxton Bullock; he had a lot of company.

But despite his fear of the big ramrod and his hatred for mustanging, he stuck out the job because of the horses. He'd saved more than one from being crippled by Paxton, and in small ways, he managed to improve their condition as much as possible. Jory suspected the ramrod understood this, perhaps allowed him to continue because he was not yet a full-grown man and worked longer hours than anyone else in the crew.

His horse taken care of, Jory sat down beside the empty corral to wait. There was no sense trying to get any sleep. When Paxton saw the mustangs were gone, he would go berserk. If he could, Jory wanted to be able to explain their good fortune before that happened. He reminded himself to tell Paxton that the quick sale had saved them at least a four-hundred mile trip to Cheyenne. No matter what Paxton thought about Mr. Buckingham, it was a break for all of them.

' Jory wished the Easterner had paid him with cash in hand. That might have made the explanation easier. But he wasn't worried. He'd bet his horse and saddle that Buckingham was good for the money.

Jory shook his head. What kind of man would throw away almost a year's wages like that? What was he doing in Running Springs? One thing sure, he *was* crazy if he thought he could go down to Nevada and change mustanging. Paxton would like that a whole bunch. The Easterner would end up feeding the coyotes. Jory wasn't one to give advice, but he resolved to try in the morning. The Easterner was a nice man, and in a strange way, he felt he owed Buckingham something because of that band of mustangs heading for the Tetons.

"Jory!"

The harsh voice jerked him erect and he felt his heart start to pound. Across the livery yard, he saw Paxton come striding at him with clenched fists.

"Now . . . now, wait a minute, Mr. Bullock!" Jory said, feeling himself backing up and not seeming to be able to stop. "Mr. Bullock, I can explain!"

Paxton stopped so close, Jory could smell the whiskey on his breath. He felt the corral poles against his back. Behind Paxton, the whole crew waited and he knew what they were waiting to see. "I sold 'em," Jory blurted. "Got two fifty each!"

Paxton's eyes narrowed. "How? To who?"

The pole grated against his spine. Jory swallowed noisily and tried to beat the fear out of his voice. It wasn't easy. Paxton's breath made him want to choke and his stare made him squirm. "To the Easterner," he stammered.

"What!"

"He bought them all, Mr. Bullock. I figured you'd be happy about it, saving us the ride to Cheyenne."

"What did he do with them, boy!"

It wasn't going to wash, Jory thought. Paxton's face was alive with unconcealed fury and his shoulder muscles tensed to swing. Strangely, the fear went out of Jory. He was going to take a beating as sure as he lived.

"What'd he do with them?" Paxton whispered menacingly.

"Turned them loose," Jory replied wearily. "We took off the wires, chains, and head sacking, then set them free."

"That a fact." Paxton stepped back, ducked his head over his shoulder and spoke to the waiting crew. "You boys hear that? The kid decided he's the one who decides things. The kid . . . needs . . . a lesson!"

Jory Parnes knew what was coming. In a split second, the thought passed through his mind that if he fought back, Paxton would beat him that much worse. And he *would* get beaten. There was no way on earth he could face up to this man. But he'd be damned if he'd stand still and take it without a fight.

He saw Paxton's head start to turn back and Jory swung away from the pole corral, his fist blurring in a tight arc. The blow jolted up through his arm and he felt his fist cramp in pain. But he staggered Paxton! The big man was off balance and caught with his hands down. If there was one advantage Jory figured he had, it was speed. So, before the ramrod could move to raise his arms, Jory hit him again, square in the mouth. Paxton roared and charged.

Jory wanted to get away. He was trying to dodge under those big, outstretched arms. If he could get clear of the fence, get out in the open where he could move—but he couldn't.

Like a claw, Paxton's hand caught him. The fingers bit into his shoulder and he stifled a cry as Paxton threw him halfway through the poles. Before he could recover, a fist exploded against his jaw and Jory pitched backward through the corral and crumpled to the dirt. He could dimly hear Paxton coming in after him and he tried to get to his feet. He grabbed the fence and started to pull himself up. Paxton's boot smashed his fingers into the wood and he cried out in pain.

Another boot caught him in the side and his mouth flew open, gasping for breath. Paxton dropped down on top of him like a building. Jory felt his hair being half ripped out of his scalp. He tried to roll, but it was hopeless. Somehow, he managed to get an arm up. He'd tear out the man's eyes if he could!

Paxton began slapping him—hard, but not as hard as he could. Jory's head jerked from side to side and blood filled his mouth and he wanted to die—or pass out. Two more blows and he did the latter.

A flush of water filled his nostrils and he started choking. "Where is it?" Paxton roared. "Where's the money!"

He tried to speak, but his lips got in the way and he felt like he couldn't breathe. Again the fingers ripped at his hair.

"Boss," a faraway voice said, "he can't tell you if he's dead. You hit him any more and he's a goner."

The fingers left his hair.

"Where is it, kid? So help me, if you don't talk, I will kill you right here and now."

Somehow, Jory managed to tell him. He couldn't see the man's face because his eyes were swollen shut and the bucket water left his vision spinning like a whirlpool.

"I'll tell you what, kid," Paxton growled, "you got a lot to learn. We have to go to Cheyenne anyway after some store-bought supplies shipped East for Hench. And we might have gotten a better deal on the mustangs, not to mention the hide men and horsemeat folks that's awaitin'. The next time you or any man tries to think for Paxton Bullock, you'd better remember this. The second lesson I give . . . is the last."

He may have passed out. He wasn't sure. For a long time, he'd lain still until the stars settled into one place and stopped jerking around in the sky. When he was finally able to roll over onto his stomach and push himself to his knees, it was almost daybreak. He crawled under the lowest pole and over to a water trough. Jory's head dropped underwater and the cold crispness stung his mashed lips and bruised face until numbness set in. When he'd removed his shirt and bathed, shivering, in the fresh, early morning air, he staggered to his feet and stood swaying like a drunk, his puffy eyes watching the first rays of the sun creeping out over the prairie.

The crew was sleeping it off inside the livery barn and that was where he'd have to go to get his gun. But the thought of shooting Paxton Bullock was only a fleeting one. He was neither killer nor fool enough to get hung. No, he decided, I'll just pack my gear and ride somewheres I've never been. He was finished with mustanging in Nevada. There wasn't a damn thing he, or the Easterner, could do to change things even a mite. At least there were a couple dozen of the wild ones who were again tasting freedom. He'd have done it all again for that much.

Jory walked stiffly into the livery. He wasn't going to ask for his past wages or anything. He didn't want people to see him with his face all swollen and discolored. Like a dog, he thought bitterly. I just want to get far away and hide until my wounds mend. His horse and saddle. That's all he needed.

He found his horse easy enough, but his saddle and bedroll were gone. His face twisted into a painful grimace and he plodded over to the sleeping form that was Paxton Bullock. It was mighty dark inside, but he could make out the big head and he stifled an urge to kick it. Instead, he nudged Paxton with his toe, saying, "Wake up."

Paxton jerked erect, reacting amazingly fast for a man with damn little sleep and a belly full of whiskey.

"I want my gear," Jory whispered. "I'm riding out."

As though nothing at all had happened the night before, Paxton yawned and said, "Take it easy, kid. You ain't been fired."

Fired! Jory's stomach knotted in cold fury. Could Paxton be such a fool as to really believe he'd stay after last night? Paxton, as though in answer, began to snore.

"Wake up!" Jory demanded, louder this time, nudging him harder.

"Goddamnit, Jory, I'm gettin' ready to climb out from under this blanket and finish last night's lesson. Now leave me alone!"

"Where's my bedroll?" Jory asked. "I'm riding."

Paxton sat up straight. There was no question about his being awake now. "You ain't riding nowhere except with us," he hissed. "What's the matter with you? There's over a month's of your back wages at the ranch."

Jory wished he had the nerve to tell Paxton what he could do with the wages. But, instead, he stood mulishly in the darkness, listening to the abnormally loud sound of his heartbeat and mumbling again about his bedroll.

Paxton swore and whipped his blankets aside. He grabbed Jory by the arm and half pulled, half shoved him outside. In the dawn's light, he looked into Jory's swollen face; he clamped his mouth on whatever he was going to say. After a long pause, he growled, "Maybe I was a little hard last night. I had a lot to drink and when you hit me . . ." He grinned suddenly, rubbed his angular jaw and thick lips. "Well, you pack a pretty good wallop for being built so jackrabbity thin."

He was trying to make a joke, make things all right again, but Jory couldn't figure out why. And he wasn't in any mood for joking. If Paxton Bullock had been drowning in a well-hole, he wouldn't drop him the water bucket.

"I still want my gear. I'm pulling out."

The smile and all attempt at appeasement evaporated. Bullock reached into his shirt pocket for the makings. Jory felt sweat form in the palms of his hands. When Paxton Bullock was cold sober and ready to strike or pull his gun, he always sought to disarm a man of any warning. Jory knew the routines, he'd seen him use this one before. Strange, Jory thought, that he'd even waste his time doing it on me. Nevertheless, Jory backed up, spotted a pitchfork to his right and grabbed it on a bound.

"You touch me again, I'll kill you, Paxton."

"Aw, you don't mean it, kid," he chuckled. But his eyes remained on the tines and he didn't move until he finished rolling his cigarette and struck a match. "I tried to tell you a minute ago that I was sorry about your face."

"You aren't sorry." Jory gripped the pitchfork so hard his

arms ached. "I don't know why you want me to stay on but . . ."

"'Cause you're good! You're the best damn bronc buster on the Hightower payroll and Hench himself knows it as well as me."

"He does?" Mr. Hightower *had* watched him break a few of the toughest ones. But the old man hadn't said anything. He didn't speak much to a common workingman. "How do you know?"

"Well, he said so! Told me plain out that you could stick a horse better'n any man he ever saw."

The pitchfork dipped in Jory's hands. Paxton casually walked a step closer.

"Stay back," Jory said quickly.

Paxton shrugged. "I hope I didn't scramble your brains last night. The way I see things, in a couple more years, Mr. Hightower sort of had you in mind for big things."

"Oh yeah?" He said it too fast. "Like what?"

"Like running a crew over near the Ruby Mountains." Paxton blew a cloud of smoke. He gazed into the distance with all the unconcern of a lizard sunning itself on a rock.

"What about you and the others?"

"I hate mustangs. You know that."

It was the first thing he'd said that Jory truly believed. "And?"

"And you have a savvy with them that I never will. I've watched you long enough to know you and I don't see things eye to eye on the way mustanging ought to be done."

"We sure don't." But Jory said it easy-like. Paxton was leading up to something. Something that made his fear wash away with excitement.

"So," Paxton grunted, "you stick with us until we get back to the ranch and I might put in a word with Mr. Hightower."

Jory's arms went slack, the pitchfork dipped in his hands. With Mr. Hightower's backing, he could . . .

Paxton moved so fast he didn't know what hit him. One

minute he was dreaming about what could be, the next moment he was stifling a cry that rose in his throat. What a fool he'd been!

Paxton grabbed him by the front of the shirt and yanked him off his feet.

"I ought to kill you," he snarled. "I oughta beat you but I already did. If you ever pull a gun or something like that pitchfork on me again, so help me I will kill you!"

He shook Jory until his teeth clattered.

"Understand?"

Jory nodded. Somehow.

Paxton shoved him away. "You're staying with my crew because I say who leaves and who don't. And if Hench didn't run things, I'd be done with you altogether."

"Then part of it was true."

"You're alive, ain't ya? The old man thinks you're about the grandest thing ever sat a saddle. He likes to see you work. So you're coming back and you'll stay on doing the only thing you'll ever be any good at. But when the day comes you get busted up too much to ride, I'll get rid of you."

Jory spat the taste of blood from his mouth. "Then the part about having my own crew up in the Ruby Mountains was a lie."

Paxton laughed and pivoted away, heading for the livery. "You better hope that Easterner pays up or you'll be working the next year for free. I'm going to hit him up pronto and if he ain't got the money, you two are going to have a matching set of faces!"

CHAPTER 3

Darby Buckingham ruefully eyed his wardrobe, which consisted of eight identical suits. Black coat, black trousers, they were tailored to his specifications by one of New York City's finest clothiers. To complete his outfit, he had four derbys and four pairs of black, round-toed shoes.

Dolly Beavers complained constantly about his lack of variety, but he didn't care. When all one's clothes were the same, it simply eliminated decisions. But as he studied his suits, he knew they wouldn't be appropriate for his journey to Nevada. He debated whether to travel by stagecoach to Elko and then buy a horse, or to take his own black gelding. It was a difficult decision. He detested the prospect of riding horseback all the way to Nevada. But even worse was the thought of attempting to find a trustworthy horse when he arrived. His own, a great, hulking beast of questionable disposition, nevertheless had managed to transport him on his past adventures. Reluctantly, he made up his mind to forsake the stage. That meant he would have to squeeze into his loathsome riding boots. His mustache drooped with disfavor.

But, despite the inconveniences, he was sure he was doing the right thing. In fact, he'd never been more certain. The experience of liberating those mustangs had left an indelible imprint on his conscience. He could use help, and had briefly entertained the notion of inviting Bear Timberly and Zack Woolsey along. But he'd discarded the idea almost as quickly as he'd hit upon it. They were just too crazy. Their first impulse was always to fight or raise hell and face the consequences later.

It was Darby's intention to study mustanging and propose some reforms he hoped a man like Hench Hightower would accept. If that failed, maybe there would be trouble, but he'd try to avoid it. That was why he was going alone. With Bear and Zack in tow, there'd be lead filling the air before he could have time to study the situation, much less begin another dime novel.

It was regrettable, he thought, that Jory Parnes hadn't accepted his offer. The young man would have been a fine source of information and assistance. He'd even thought Jory felt the way he did about Hightower's methods. Darby shrugged philosophically; maybe he was a fool getting involved in something about which he knew nothing. But he did know one thing when he saw it—unrestrained cruelty.

During the next hour, he loaded his suitcases, which he would send by stagecoach to Elko. The saddlebags were too small to hold much, but he stuffed them as full as he could. He took special care to cushion two dozen Cuban cigars between his underclothes; with luck, they would be safe. But, just in case, he dug out a sack of tobacco and cigarette papers. He knew how to roll his own, but only as a last resort. In a final gesture of self-indulgence, Darby stuffed in two bottles of the finest French brandy money could buy and one crystal snifter. To make room, he had to leave six pairs of socks, but with the high-topped cowboy boots, no one would notice if his feet stank anyway. When it came down to a choice between satisfying one's palate or one's feet, it was a pretty simple judgment.

"Yoo-hoo, Derby dear. It's me. Open up."

"Blast!" he muttered, vainly searching for a place to hide that didn't exist. When she saw him in boots with his suitcases packed, there was going to be an unpleasant scene. "Blast!"

He heard the familiar sound of passkey in his door lock. It was too early for a drink, but he had the feeling he was going to need one before she left. "Come in, Miss Beavers," he sighed.

"Oh, Derby. . . ."

"Darby," he corrected automatically. "When *will* you remember!"

But she wasn't listening. Her big, blue eyes stared at his suitcases, then widened further when she saw the boots. Her hand flew to her mouth in an involuntary motion and the chronic happy smile she wore evaporated.

"Darby?"

When she was shaken, he noticed, she could speak his name correctly. But he didn't tell her that; she already looked distressed enough. His heart softened and he suddenly felt almost guilty for leaving. But if it hadn't been for Dolly, he'd have gone some time ago. Still, this was what she'd always dreaded and there was no easy way to face her now.

"Dolly," he began, "I'm going away, but I'll be back."

"Where?" she breathed. "When! Oh, Darby, no!"

With a charge like a great, white Prussian broodmare, Dolly slammed into him, flattening them on the bed. Only this time, her intentions weren't the least bit amorous.

"When are you leaving?" she whispered.

"This morning."

"Is it because of those horses? Are you going to Nevada?"

"Yes."

"I want to go."

"No."

She didn't argue. She didn't protest. And he loved her for it. Dolly just rolled off him and stared bleakly at his luggage and fought back tears.

He felt like a murderer. He slid off the bed and poured a stiff one, taking it neat in a single gulp. "Now, Dolly, please don't cry. You know I can't stand that. And I'll be returning in a couple of months."

"Months!" If anything, her face went even whiter.

He resolved to try harder. "Dolly, it must be four hundred miles to Elko. It will take me two weeks just to get there." What a horrible thought that was. He'd better pack another bottle and at least another dozen Cubans, he thought. Maybe he'd sell the gelding and take the stage back. A month in the saddle was extraordinarily harsh.

"Are Bear and Zack going along?"

"They would if I asked," he said. "But they've got their own hotel to watch just as you do."

Dolly nodded silently. She passed by and stood looking out the window. "I'll never rent the John C. Frémont suite to anyone after you. I mean it."

"Oh come now," he said soothingly. "I'll be back in a couple of months and everything will be fine."

"No you won't," she said decisively. "You came West in search of adventures to write about and you can't do that by spending time in Running Springs. Once you reach Elko and straighten out this horse business, you'll want to keep going."

He wanted to tell her it wasn't true, but he couldn't. There was a gold and silver boom going on in a place called Virginia City. Apparently, the discovery was even greater than the forty-niner gold rush in California. He wanted to see it, be there when historic events occurred. During the past year, there hadn't been a week that didn't bring men passing through town on the way to the Comstock Lode. And San Francisco, they said it was . . .

"Darby." She'd interrupted his thoughts. "Darby, I can see that traveling look in your eye. If it hadn't been those mustangs, something else would have pulled you away from me."

He frowned, knowing she was right.

"Do you love me?" she whispered, so softly he barely heard her.

He shifted uneasily. He should have gone before sunrise and left a note.

"Darby!" She knelt down beside him, took his flat-knuckled, fighter's hands in her own. She spoke to the hands. "Darby, I have to know the truth before you go.

Now, I realize you're not a man who . . . who says how he feels, but I have to know. Do you love me?"

Blast! He took a deep breath. The air seemed stifling. He thought about it for almost a minute before he said, "Yes, Dolly, I believe I do."

"Wa-hee!" she screeched. She leapt from the floor and bent his short neck back and began kissing wildly. Once again, he found himself struggling to get free but he was saved by a loud knock at the door.

"Damn," Dolly panted.

"Whew," he sighed. "Who is it?"

"Paxton Bullock. I came for my money. Let me in."

Darby pushed up from the bed and snatched a handkerchief from his pocket. He wiped away Dolly's lipstick as best he could. When he opened the door, Paxton was standing with his hands on his hips, looking very out of sorts. His bloodshot eyes swept by Darby and passed over the woman and crumpled bedspread. A smug grin came to his lips and Darby understood its meaning.

"I was going to bring the money over personally."

"Sure. But the lady sort of sidetracked you. I understand."

Darby's mustache bristled. He would have liked to have flattened this grinning idiot. But he decided to let it pass.

"You owe me one hundred twenty-five dollars," Paxton grunted. "Cash."

Darby wheeled, almost tripping and falling in the unaccustomed high-heeled boots. He strode over to his coat and ripped his wallet free. In a secret compartment, he always kept a one-hundred-dollar bill. The rest was normal carrying money.

"I see you're packing. Going back East where you belong, huh?"

Darby replaced the wallet and smiled menacingly. "As a matter of fact," he said, "I'm traveling west."

Paxton tried to sound offhand, but it didn't quite come out right. "Business or pleasure?"

"Business," Darby replied, starting to enjoy the expression on Paxton's face. "I might go into business around Elko. Your territory, I believe."

"What kind of business?" The leering grin was definitely missing now.

Darby thought it over. After a moment, he decided he might as well give Paxton something to chew on for a few weeks. "I'm thinking about going mustanging," he said quietly.

Paxton's jaw dropped. He seemed to be trying to decide if it was some kind of a joke. He closed his gaping mouth and the jaw muscles corded along his cheeks. He'd apparently decided the Easterner wasn't joking at all. "Mister," he gritted, "you'd better put away those duds of yours and stay here where you got friends to watch out for you. In Elko, things are different. You could say they're a whole lot less healthy for strangers who come messing into things they shouldn't."

"Thanks for the advice," Darby said easily, "but I think I'll go anyway. You see, I am a writer and I smell a story over there." He paused, almost able to see the wheels turning in the big ramrod's head.

"What kind of story?" Paxton clipped.

"Oh, I don't think you'd want to hear it."

"Try me, goddamnit!"

Darby shrugged. "All right. It's a story about men who hunt horses. That in itself should be exciting, don't you think?"

"Hell no, it ain't. It's just hard, dangerous work."

"Well," Darby said, glancing over at Dolly and winking conspiratorially, "it must have a lot of fine moments I can include. Like the thrill of putting a rifle slug through the skull of a running stallion."

Paxton's face flushed with blood. He looked as if he were going to gag.

Darby pushed on. "Or how you run them down with relay teams until they sometimes crash to the desert floor with exploded hearts. Or perhaps how you keep them away from water day after day in the heat of summer. Yes, that would be exciting, reading about you watching their tongues swell up . . ."

"Enough!" Paxton's fists were balled and he looked ready to charge. A big vein stood out on his neck and throbbed. He was so furious he had trouble speaking. "You . . . you come and write that . . . that . . ."

"What?"

Paxton yanked his gun. Darby's heart missed a beat and he heard a sharp intake of breath from Dolly. But the ramrod just cocked back the hammer and spun the cylinder as if checking his load.

"You know," he said, eying the weapon critically, "I've been handling guns all my life. Most always, I can hit anything I aim at. Hell, I've blown sparrows out of the air and that's shooting." His voice dropped. "But once in a while, I'll draw my six-shooter and miss entirely."

"That's a shame," Darby said, uncertain as to what the man was driving at.

"Sure is," Paxton grinned, "'cause when I miss, the bullet is likely to hit anything. Just a wild bullet flying . . . flying who knows where. It can accidentally hit someone. Someone big, like yourself even. Course our sheriff, he understands how accidents like that can happen. Can't hardly arrest a man for something like that. It's just one of them things that happen. Too damn bad. Savvy?"

Darby nodded and watched Paxton slap the gun back into his holster. The warning was all too clear, but came as no surprise. He'd known since the minute he saw Paxton draw his gun yesterday in the street that this man was capable, even eager, to kill. Without question Darby knew that if he went to Elko, the day would come when he'd have to handle Paxton. If he could. The ramrod came with the territory, right along with rattlesnakes, scorpions, and a man named Hench Hightower.

"I understand," Darby said. "However, accidents can be

prevented. Sometimes all it takes is to remove a potential danger."

Before Paxton could react, Darby switched the subject and caught him off balance. "Tell Jory Parnes I'll be along after breakfast. I want to talk to him again."

"Forget it. Jory don't want to talk to you."

"Why?" Darby asked bluntly.

"Because he made a mistake selling those horses without my saying so. But Jory's a real smart boy. And after I showed him his mistake, he realized how wrong it was. I guess you could say the lesson he learned left a real impression on the kid. One he won't forget."

"I don't understand," Darby said in puzzlement. "He told me that you'd be happy because it would save everyone a trip to Cheyenne."

"Well," Paxton drawled, "Jory was wrong. In a lot of ways. But he didn't know we have to ride over to Cheyenne anyway and it could be we might have been able to get a few more dollars at the market."

"That's crazy!" Darby snapped. "Half those mustangs wouldn't even have survived that long."

"Maybe yes, maybe no. But it was my decision, not Jory's." He tipped his hat at Dolly. "Nice to see a good lookin' woman all flushed and havin' fun."

Before Darby could reach him, Paxton slammed the door and was gone and Dolly was holding him by the arm.

"It's all right," she said. "Let him go."

Darby shook his head. He was going to tear that man apart.

"Darby. If you are going this morning . . ." Her words trailed off. She *was* a little flushed. He forgot about Paxton almost instantly.

Darby eyed the gelding with apprehension and wished that the onlookers would vanish. Bear and Zack had donated a pack horse and outfit for the trip. Bedroll, pots, pans, coffee, beans, dried jerky, a few books, and some extra clothes. Even now, they were still adding things. If they didn't stop, he'd be mistaken for a traveling dry-goods store.

"That's enough," Darby said.

"Aw, come on," Zack grouched, "you need a hatchet to cut firewood, don't you?"

"Well . . . maybe so." He hadn't thought about that.

"Then take this 'un."

"That's an ax!"

"So the handle will stick out a mite. What about taking one of our buffalo rifles?" Zack asked hopefully.

"The shotgun will do," Darby answered. Already the pack horse was starting to look shakey-legged under the load it carried.

"Buckingham, you can't draw down on wild game with a shotgun. Even if you hit anything, you'd blow it to smithereens. And when you ate the meat, you'd swallow so many pellets you'd never get back into the saddle!"

They began to guffaw, the two old hunters slapping each other on the back and raising enough racket to attract the whole town.

He had to get going. Darby considered the stirrup. The gelding was too tall and his legs were too short but he desperately wanted to make a decent show of it for Dolly's sake. Somehow, he managed to get a toehold and stretched for the saddle horn. With a tremendous heave, he left the ground and the gelding almost fell over as it began crabbing sideways for balance. For a second, he wasn't sure if it was going to work, but the animal regained its footing and he was up. Bear and Zack, however, were down, rolling with hysterical laughter.

"Good-by, Dolly," he said stiffly.

"Darby? Will I see you again?"

"Of course." He ignored the two old hunters and beckoned her closer. "Listen," he whispered, "if it will make you feel any better, I'll write when I reach Elko. Don't worry, I'll see you again."

She squeezed his knee painfully and he saw she was on

the verge of crying. It was definitely time to ride. "So long, Bear, Zack."

Still in the dirt, they stopped laughing. "Damn," Bear muttered, suddenly very subdued. "We sure wish we was riding along with you."

"Well, you can't. You both have a business to run, if you remember. But if I need any assistance, I'll send a wire. I just wish that young bronc rider, Jory Parnes, had joined me. He would have been helpful."

Bear scrubbed his jaw. "Not likely. I was out in the alley emptying whiskey bottles when they rode by. Didn't hardly recognize that young pup."

"What do you mean?" Darby asked, his attention riveted to Bear.

"Well, the kid was all beat to hell and he could hardly sit his horse. Looked like he musta got on the wrong end of a mother moose, he was so banged up."

Darby didn't say a word. One of his promises to Dolly was that he'd go to Elko, hire a crew, and stay out of trouble. Now, he couldn't let her know that he was breaking that promise. Just as soon as he rode west, out of sight, he would circle back toward Cheyenne. With any luck, he'd catch them before nightfall, tomorrow at the latest. There wasn't a doubt in his mind who had worked Jory over. Paxton had to outweigh that kid by nearly a hundred pounds. Darby figured it would be interesting to see how the ramrod fared against a man as big as himself.

He pried Dolly's fingers from his leg and waved good-by. As he bounced out of Running Springs, he didn't look back. His mind was on Paxton Bullock.

CHAPTER 4

Darby rode west until he was certain no one in Running Springs could see him any longer. Then he began to circle back, keeping a line of cottonwood trees between himself and the town. The black gelding, truculent and resentful at the prospect of carrying his heavy weight, picked up its pace as soon as he changed to the general direction of town. Several times Darby had to jerk the horse out of a bone-jarring trot that sent him bouncing from the saddle with every stride. Before he'd ridden five miles, his trousers were continually inching up around his knees and chafing angry rashes. There was no way he could avoid the discomfort the first few days of long hours in the saddle would bring.

Had it not been for Jory Parnes, he would have started the journey at a leisurely pace. But the thought of the young man, beaten and probably in even worse pain than himself, made Darby push hard.

He wasn't sure what he'd do or say when he caught up with the Hightower mustangers. But it seemed likely that he'd have to whip Paxton Bullock. He was sure he could do it if he got the chance. What had him worried, though, was the likelihood that Paxton would start shooting before Darby could get within arm's reach.

As the hours passed, Darby considered several approach strategies. One was to get in front of the riders and step out from cover as they rode by. The idea was to be among them before Paxton had a chance to react. But the more he thought about it, the dumber the plan seemed. It took less than a second for a gunman to draw and fire. No matter how close he managed to get, it wouldn't be close enough. Per-

haps he could sneak in at night? This seemed a more intelli-
gent method at first. But the problem was, in the dark, he
wouldn't be able to tell who was who. And he could hardly
go around waking up the wrong people. Besides, nights on
the prairie were for sleeping rather than crawling about half-
blind.

In the end, he decided the best chance he had was to ride
up boldly and hope to talk his way close enough to Bullock
that he could punch him out of the saddle if need be. Once
he accomplished that much, he couldn't even try to predict
what would happen. Paxton's men might interfere or they
might stay out of a fair fight. And what about Jory? It was
possible the kid wouldn't even want help. Maybe he was
used to being treated as brutally as the Nevada mustangs he
seemed to love. There was just no way of guessing until he
caught them. All Darby knew for sure was that he had to
find out if Jory was with Paxton by choice or not.

At sunset, Darby could ride no farther. He was exhausted
and the gelding had definitely won the first round. Darby
was so stiff he could barely lift his leg over the saddle, and
he eased to solid ground with a deep sigh of relief. He found
two pairs of stout hobbles and managed to apply them to
both horses. His greatest fear was that the gelding and pack
horse would bolt and run away, leaving him afoot on the
prairie. It would be a long walk back to Running Springs
and arriving horseless would be worse than humiliating.

Darby unsaddled both the animals with a Wyoming sunset burning the mountains shades of salmon and gold. He
led his horses to a spring and pointed out to them a meadow
where the grass was lush. That finished, he peeled away his
black coat and not-so-white shirt and kicked his boots off
before collapsing against the trunk of a tree. He intended to
rest for only a moment, but fell asleep with his derby still
on.

He woke up in the night, shivering cold and so stiff he
could barely unbend. Far to the east, a thin grayness edged
the world and he suspected it was less than an hour until

daybreak. There was no sense trying to go back to sleep. He needed warmth and food. Coffee, too. Scalding and black and strong enough to match his Cuban cigars.

As he dressed and gathered wood for a small campfire, the thought occurred that he was ill-suited for the rugged, outdoor life. He was a creature of comfort, a connoisseur of legendary wines and gastronomic delectabilities. He wondered if his eastern readership would ever fully appreciate what he went through in the name of authenticity. Probably not.

He cooked his breakfast of beans and dried beef, and washed it down with an entire pot of coffee. As the sun slipped over the mountains, he scrubbed his cooking utensils and shaved in cold creek water, grimacing all the while.

In a small pool, he studied his reflection. And it came to him then that he had to abandon his city attire. Already his coat was rumpled and unkempt-looking. The derby he wore offered no protection from the sun, the white shirt was turning gray, and his trousers rode up too high on his legs when he rode. All the previous day, they'd crept above his boot tops, bunching at his knees until they had rubbed the insides of his legs sore. The coat was too thin to offer any warmth at night and his face was nicked from shaving.

Right then he made a monumental decision. Darby stood up and glared down at his watery image. With a sigh, he concluded that, if he were going to live like a barbarian for the next few weeks, he might as well look like one. In his pack, Bear Timberly had shoved a complete set of buckskins that would more or less fit. Yesterday, he'd been indulgent enough to let the old hunter insist that he take them along. Today, he was ready to admit the leather breeches, fringed jacket, wide-brimmed flat hat, and heavy buffalo-hide overcoat was what he needed.

He shivered out of his eastern duds and into the buckskins. Despite Bear's great size, they were still a little tight, but he knew he'd be losing weight fast during the next few weeks. And they did feel good. Really good. The leather was soft, beautifully tanned, and, most remarkable, clean. The shirt was a little long in the arms, and the fringes hung below his hands, but he rolled up the sleeves into cuffs. Bear had also provided some moccasins, but they were way too big, so he left his boots on. Even in his high heels, the pants were still a trifle long.

He returned to the pool of water and studied himself from head to foot. His mouth lifted at the corners as he removed his derby and replaced it with the wide-brimmed leather hat. He stared at the reflection, and after a long moment, he chuckled out loud, in obvious approval. It wasn't bad, not bad at all. When he let his beard grow out, he'd be as un-tamed-looking as any mountain man. He'd be a phony, al-most totally ignorant of the wilds, but he sure looked le-gitimate. The transformation had been remarkable. So remarkable no one would—that was it! The way he'd get close enough to Paxton. The man wouldn't recognize him, until it was too late.

In five minutes, Darby rode his horse at a gallop out of the trees, his pack horse struggling to keep up. Time was wasting and Darby wanted to catch the men he followed this very morning.

He discovered their camp less than two hours later. A cir-cle of rocks containing dying coals was easily spotted on the prairie. The men and horses left a trail even he could follow without difficulty. The tracks swung south, climbing into higher country and leaving the prairie. Darby pushed on, forcing his horses into a jog that he'd been told was, al-though uncomfortable, the best way to cover ground fast without winding your mount.

The tracks circled a tall peak, and he had to go more slowly because of the rocks. Big pines reached toward the blue Wyoming skies and the mountains began to crowd him. In forest, he noticed things were somehow quieter and the only sounds were those of his horses' feet and their laboring breath as the terrain grew ever more rugged.

How far was he behind now? Each time he came to an

opening in the trees, Darby reined up and studied the land-scape ahead. But nothing moved. He wished he knew more about reading track. Bear or Zack would be able to tell how close they were, just by the freshness of the hoof prints. Yet, the coals had been alive and the gasping of his horses led him to be sure he'd been pushing as hard as possible. Still, his animals were as fat as prairie dogs and as out of shape as himself. Perhaps he was even falling behind.

But it was only twenty minutes later when he saw them. Up ahead. Through the trees. Watering their horses in a clear mountain stream.

Darby wrenched the gelding sideways off the trail, liter-ally dragging the pack horse behind. He dismounted in heavy timber. A horse whinnied and the pack animal jerked up its head, staring, nostrils dilated. Darby lunged, clamp-ing a hand over the animal's muzzle. "Please," he whis-pered, "shut up!"

When he was sure the urge had passed, he released his hold and tied the horse to a stout bush. Then he hauled him-self back onto the gelding and started circling through the trees. He had to get ahead of them, his plan depended on that.

After what seemed like a long time but could have been no more than fifteen minutes, he was in position. They would have to pass this way and he'd be ready. But it had been close. A few of the riders were back in the saddle and big Paxton was one of them. Darby knew they'd be arriving in minutes.

He tied the gelding nearby and studied the ground for a moment. Then, he reached into his saddlebags and rum-maged around until he found one of the brandy bottles and his derringer. Quickly, he uncorked the bottle, took a long pull and forced himself to pour most of the precious con-tents into the pine needles that carpeted the mountainside.

With the sound of hoofs striking rocks close by, he flopped down on his back, balanced the derringer on his lips, and slapped the big leather hat over his face. Then he stretched his arms out from his sides so there could be no suspicion of danger. The only thing he held was the empty bottle. With his heart pounding, he forced himself to lie still and wait. It wouldn't be long.

The sound of creaking leather was so loud he almost jerked. Under the hat, the derringer started to slide and he worked his lips frantically to keep it in place.

"Well, look what we got here!"

The voice was unmistakably that of Paxton Bullock. And it was close.

"A mountain man at work," someone said, and Darby heard laughter. He was just about to reach for the derringer when another said, "What are you going to do, Paxton?"

A stirrup leather creaked and Paxton said, "Reckon I'll just see that he isn't all weighted down with money. Just stay in them saddles, boys. Won't take but a minute."

A boot prodded him roughly. "Hey, mister. Wake up!"

Darby grunted incoherently.

This time Paxton kicked him. Hard.

Darby grimaced and raised his hand shakily, and there wasn't a man watching who didn't think the sleeper was just reaching to uncover his face. But the hand slipped under the hat, clenched the derringer.

"I said . . ." Paxton's voice died in his throat.

Darby sat up with the derringer aimed not two feet from the big ramrod's gaping mouth.

"You've said more than I want to hear," Darby growled.

Paxton swallowed noisily.

"Drop your gun with your left hand, Bullock." He glanced at the riders. "If anyone moves for his weapon, I'll pull the trigger."

Paxton's eyes widened. "Do as he says."

Darby watched as the big, roughhewn horseman carefully unholstered his weapon and dropped it. "Step back," he said softly.

Paxton did as he was told. But the surprise was over, and

in its place, came anger. "You!" he spat. "I should have known from the size. What do you want?"

"First, I'll talk to Jory Parnes."

From the back of the group, Jory rode forward.

Darby gritted his teeth when he saw the battered face. One eye was swollen shut and the kid's lips were purplish. Darby's hand began to tremble and the derringer danced.

"Watch out with that gun," Paxton blurted. "You look crazy enough to use it."

"I am," Darby whispered. "Any second I may have one of those 'accidents' you talked about in Running Springs. Remember?"

Paxton just nodded, his eyes fixed on the derringer. It held only one bullet but it was a .44 caliber and that was big enough to stop any man at close range.

"Mr. Buckingham, you shouldn't have come after me," Jory said.

"That's my decision. Now I want yours. The offer still holds, only I'd forgotten to tell you I'll pay you three times what Mr. Hightower does. But instead of catching mustangs his way, we'll try something different."

Everyone was watching Jory, as though his answer held some kind of signal. Darby wished he were holding the shotgun instead of a derringer.

"Jory, if you ride out on us, you better keep going," Paxton gritted.

Jory looked frantic. "I honest to God wish you hadn't come, Mr. Buckingham. I don't know what's going to happen to you. But I got back wages waitin' in Elko and I signed on for the job. I ain't no quitter."

"Quitter!" Darby swore. "Just what *do* you think you are? A slave? Wake up, Jory. If it's the back wages, I know Paxton here will pay you right now. Isn't that right?"

"Go to hell, mister!"

Darby's neck seemed to drop into his round shoulders.

Even if he'd wasted his time on Jory, there was something to be gained by repaying this man for beating the kid and for his cruel handling of those mustangs.

Darby tossed the derringer aside and raised his fists. Paxton blinked as if he couldn't believe his eyes. In the next instant, he showed what he was made of. He dove for his gun.

Darby caught him squarely in the jaw with a wicked upper-cut that lifted him off his feet and laid him out on the pine needles with the gun skidding out of reach.

"Get up," Darby said tonelessly.

Paxton jumped to his feet and began to circle. His eyes were wild, his knuckles white and broad. He was at least four inches taller than Darby, with a definite advantage in reach. But their weights were close. Buckingham was five feet nine inches and shaped like the stump of an oak tree. At two hundred fifty-five pounds, he carried only fifteen pounds of fat. That fifteen pounds was immeasurably deceptive. The rest was all muscle and bone.

Paxton jabbed. Darby blocked with ease. Paxton feigned another jab, then followed with a haymaker. Darby slipped underneath and caught him at the point of his rib cage, just under the breastbone. The ramrod's face went gray and his eyes almost popped. Darby backed up, giving the man time to recover. There was no expression on the writer's face. Neither elation, nor anger, nor pity. If anything, there was simply a fighter's concentration to do a job and do it well. In this role, there were few men better. For he'd once fought for a crown, won, and fought again. Despite his sophistication, he knew every trick of the most savage New York street fighter because he'd been one, long ago. In his youth, he had been beaten. As a man, never. With his writing came financial security and the end of his fight career.

But now, it all came back as he'd known it would. The timing, the instinctive blocking of punches, slipping and moving.

"Don't quit now," he graveled, "we are just beginning."

Paxton charged, trying to wrap his arms around Darby. He stepped sideways and connected over the ear with a punch that sent the man reeling. Again Darby let him recover.

Paxton whirled, charged again. This time, the layer of pine needles slipped from under Darby's feet and the ramrod brought up a vicious knee kick that knocked the Easterner sprawling. Paxton was better with his feet than with his hands. Before Darby could scramble erect, the big mustanger drove a boot in his ribs, then reared back and kicked again. Darby managed to grab ahold of the boot and he twisted it violently.

But the cowboy landed on top. Darby reached up, grabbed him by the throat, and shook him. Paxton's head snapped back and forth and there was a look of terror in his eyes. A strong man himself, his arms were half the size of Darby's and totally ineffective. Darby tossed him aside and jumped to his feet.

"Come on," he said, "we're not finished."

Paxton was on one knee, his head down. He looked beat. He pushed himself erect and stood swaying, trying to get his breath. Darby let him. He glanced over at Jory Parnes and knew that the score wasn't yet even. He thought about the wild horses, and his mustache bristled with hatred.

Paxton must have seen that and known he had no chance. "Rope him, boys! Rope and drag 'im!" he cried hoarsely.

Before Darby could move, they were spurring their horses into him, shaking out ropes. Suddenly, they peeled off and the ropes started coming at him. He batted them away; he stepped through loops. One rider managed to catch him, dallied on his saddle horn, and started to turn his horse. Darby charged, got ahold of his leg and tore him out of his saddle. But that took a precious second or two, and he could feel more loops settling over his shoulders. One tightened around his neck before he could tear it free. There was a tremendous jerk and he couldn't breathe. His hands came up and he tried to rip it away. He was like a blind, savage, and wounded animal. He staggered around under the trees, feeling the ropes settle over him, the terrible jerking as horses pulled in every direction, threatening to rip him apart.

With the blood pounding in his ears, he still heard Paxton screaming orders, laughing like a crazy man. Once, when Darby caught a swirling glimpse of him, he reached out, trying desperately to get his fingers onto the man. He'd kill Paxton before the ropes strangled him. But he couldn't quite reach him and he was being yanked violently back and forth. There was no hope at all. Paxton moved in, swinging. The blows were slow, deliberate, destructive. Darby fell to his knees, his fingers trying to pull the noose from his neck. If only he could breathe, regain strength, if only. . . .

The rope at his throat suddenly went slack. Three shots blanked the air and Jory Parnes was standing beside him with a Winchester rifle pointed at Paxton Bullock. Jory Parnes, with tears streaming down his face—a face as white and deathly-looking as monument marble.

Everything stopped. The ropes loosened. A sudden movement and the Winchester swung sideways barking twice and Darby, his eyes watery and unfocusing, heard the unmistakable sound of two riders hitting the earth. The Winchester was back on target. The long muzzle pointed squarely at Bullock's heart.

"Do it," Jory rasped. "Go ahead and make a move so I can kill you!"

A diamondback rattlesnake could have been crawling up his boot top and Paxton wouldn't have flinched. He didn't even breathe.

"Back wages," Jory panted. "Sixty dollars. Now!"

Out came the money. The boss didn't bother to count change.

"Now, load up Don and Red and get the hell out of here!"

"You murdered them," Paxton said.

But Jory shook his head. "Take a look. They've both got guns in their hands. Now git."

Paxton was no fool. He could see Jory was in a mind to kill and that he was the prime candidate. He mounted his horse and spurred away. At the edge of cover, he viciously yanked his horse into a slide and spun it around tight.

"We'll get you, Jory. You and him. You're both dead men the day you ride into Nevada. Dead men!"

It was several minutes before Darby attempted speech. His thick neck was crisscrossed with raw, fleshy rope burns and Paxton's fists had torn one eyebrow badly and left his face almost as swollen and battered as Jory's. They were quite a pair and Darby dryly made mention of the fact.

Jory smiled but said nothing. His eyes drifted down toward the trail where the Hightower crew had run.

"Are you sorry about taking my side?" Darby asked, trying to fathom the young man's thoughts.

Jory shook his head. "Nope. I was just thinking about all of it and trying to understand." He hesitated. "I've worked with that crew a long time and I'd figured that, if it wasn't for Paxton, most of them would be a pretty decent bunch. Even when they roped you, I was sure that they might rough you up pretty good, then let you go."

Jory's eyes swung up to meet Darby's and there was pain and confusion in his face. "They were going to choke you to death!" he cried brokenly. "I . . . I kept waiting for them to call it off but they . . . they didn't."

"So you saved my life," Darby said. "Is it so surprising? You alone of all those men had the compassion to help ease the suffering of the mustangs. It's character, Jory. And you've got it."

Jory fidgeted self-consciously. "Seems to me you're loaded with this 'character' yourself."

Darby scowled. Pretty quick, they were going to be making speeches for each other. It was time to change the subject, face up to a couple of hard decisions. "Are you any good with a gun?"

Jory pursed his lips thoughtfully, then shook his head.

"Nope. I can hit what I aim at with a rifle." He sighed. "You saw the proof of that. Two dead men."

"What about a handgun?"

"Never used one much. I can't draw, if that's what you mean. Can you?"

"No," Darby growled. "I've tried but it's hopeless. It seems to me that if we run into Paxton in Elko he would be fully capable of drawing and shooting us both dead in the street."

"He would, for a fact, Mr. Buckingham."

"Call me Darby."

"I heard in town they call you the Derby Man. That because of those fancy duds you was wearing?"

He glanced down at the buckskins and smiled wryly. "I suppose so. Listen, Jory. You saved my life and I won't insult you by offering repayment. But I will give you some advice."

"I'm a good listener. Go on."

"I think you'd be better off making a start somewhere other than Nevada."

"What about the mustangs?"

"There must be other states where you could find them."

"Sure," Jory said, a hint of impatience in his voice, "but I don't much like the idea of anyone telling me a whole damned state is off limits. Now, maybe you ought to listen to your own advice."

"Don't be ridiculous," Darby snapped, "no Buckingham ever ran from trouble."

"Well, neither did a Parnes!" The young man's jaw was set, determined. "If you can't draw a gun then I'm going to have to learn in one big hurry, mister. 'Cause the day will come when we run into Bullock and I'd better be ready. Starting today, I'm going to be practicing all the time."

"With what?" Darby exclaimed. "You aren't even wearing one."

"There's a gun and holster in my saddlebag." Jory dug it out for him. Darby eyed the weapon suspiciously. "Looks pretty well shot to me. No pun intended," he said quickly.

"It's old, all right. Probably weighs a pound more than most handguns."

"The holster looks rotten. I don't see how you can even get the gun out."

Jory's expression clouded. He lifted his right hand up and stared at his palm in a strange way. After a moment, he said, "I'm not sure how I'll do it. But there *has* to be a way." The fingers clenched slowly and whatever deep thoughts had been his faded. "Don't worry. That gun will hit what it points at. I reckon it will do."

"For a while," Darby said. "First big town we ride into, I'm going to purchase you the best holster weapon I can buy. But I don't want to have to stop back in Running Springs. Personal reasons."

"A woman?" Jory asked, apparently eager to change the conversation.

Darby nodded.

"That's what I thought. They sure can cause a fella some grief, can't they."

"So, you've learned that much, have you. Then you must know more."

Jory blushed, forgot about his swollen eye, and tried to wink. He grimaced instead. "We'd sure scare 'em off the way we look."

Darby pressed a finger to his torn eyebrow. There was old scar tissue there from his fighting days. That was probably why it ripped.

"Let's get riding," Darby said. "I want to get back to my pack horse and make camp. I've got one bottle of brandy left and some good cigars we can share."

"Don't smoke or drink," Jory said.

"That's good," Darby grunted. "I didn't bring enough to last us both anyway."

A few minutes later, Jory pushed back his stetson and said, "You always get on your horse from off a rock?"

Darby scowled his blackest. "Only when I can find one," he rumbled. "Let's ride. I have a feeling it's going to be a long trip."

CHAPTER 5

They did not become close friends at once. But, as the days passed, Darby sensed a strong fellowship beginning to develop. Jory Parnes had a quick and ready mind, and unlike some western men he had met, a genuine curiosity about the world beyond his own. At night around the campfire, Darby found a willing listener, eager to learn about the East and countries of Europe he knew he would never see.

Jory's formal education was sadly lacking. Like most cowboys, he'd started working at an early age and could barely write much more than his name. Always a man with a handy sheet of paper and a stock of ink and quills, Darby, without stating it, began to teach Jory how to read and write.

But, during the day, it was Jory who did the teaching. Darby was constantly amazed at his knowledge of trees and vegetation, horses, cattle, wildlife, and even geology. Jory understood basic concepts of how mountains and valleys were formed. And though he didn't use the scientific names, he could identify almost everything they saw.

When Darby pressed him for the basis of his knowledge, Jory told him that cowboys were as diverse a group of men as you'd meet anywhere. They came, he said, from eastern cities, the bayous of the South, from Europe and even from Africa. Most were rootless, wandering men who traveled on foot and on horseback. They were the kind of men who left good jobs—and sometimes good women, too—just for the hell of it.

That was his education, and Darby Buckingham realized that, while formal schooling gave the basics to a young mind, it was the quality of that mind that ultimately decided how much would be learned. And, as in Jory's case, sometimes the lack of formal schooling was scarcely more than a minor shortcoming. With curiosity and intelligence, an uneducated man could even become a scholar, in the ways he needed to be.

As for his upbringing, Jory didn't seem to want to talk about it and Darby never pressed. But there were small bits of information that, when totaled, formed a tale of an unhappy childhood. His father had died in a mine cave-in up in the Colorado mountains and his mother remarried. Jory's stepfather was a much older man, a man with his own sons full-grown. They'd barely tolerated each other until Jory was fourteen, then he'd ridden off. He figured it was better for all of them.

Despite his youth, the young man was an encyclopedia of knowledge when it came to wild horses. Later at night, when the campfire was no more than a bed of glowing coals and it was impossible to read the letters and words that Jory struggled to master, they talked of those horses. Darby learned of their social order, how the stallions would fight for their mares, drive them with teeth and hoofs when threatened. There was nothing, Jory said, more dangerous than a captured stallion. They would attack a man or, failing that chance, kill themselves in an attempt for freedom. They were often shot and run off cliffs, but every year there were new ones fighting for mares, seemingly faster, stronger, and smarter than their predecessors.

The first time most cowboys saw a stallion racing free across the desert or scrambling up rocky slopes that seemed impossible to climb, Jory said the feeling was almost universal—they wanted the horse. He remembered one famous stallion that was so magnificent that the best mustangers from all over the West came to try and settle their loops over his head. He was a palomino and became known as Golden Boy. One particular rancher, a man by the name of Abe Patterson, used a crew of more than a dozen men every spring, and again in the fall, trying to catch that horse. And finally, after three years of studying his habits, they found a small, almost undetectable canyon where Golden Boy drove his mares when he was pressed into desperation. And on an October morning, they caught him.

Surprisingly, he didn't fight the rope much. Not much at all. And, when a visibly shaking bronc buster swung into the saddle, Golden Boy only trembled. He learned the cues and manners of a fine pleasure horse almost immediately. Everyone said the great palomino must have once been a saddle horse.

Patterson was delighted, so the story went. Every chance, he rode Golden Boy into town just to show him off. That stallion was the rancher's pride. It was almost eight months later that Patterson happened to be riding alone and dismounted at a small desert spring. Golden Boy waited until he was stretched out to drink—and then he stomped the rancher to death, burying him in the thick, oozing mud.

No, Jory told him. You could whip them, work them to skeletons, castrate them even—but some day they would turn and kill you if they could. Just like Paxton Bullock.

The man was never far from their thoughts. And Jory, true to his word, practiced his draw constantly. Over and over, a hundred times for each mile ridden, he drew the old .36 caliber Navy Colt. But he never pulled the trigger and his speed never improved. Darby couldn't understand why. Perhaps it was the gun. It seemed huge in Jory's hand and cumbersome to the extreme. Darby wished he knew more about the art of gunfighting. Once, Sheriff Zeb Cather, still considered to be one of the fastest men alive, had demonstrated to him the basics of the draw. Darby tried to pass this along as well as he could.

He remembered that Zeb never actually aimed his weapon, but rather pointed it from waist high. That was for the quick draw when a man was in tight spaces or up close. On the stand-up draw, Zeb kind of shifted his right foot forward so that he was standing sideways toward his target.

The old lawman swore that this stance had saved his life more than once.

But what made Zeb the professional he was really centered around something inside that tightened down and made him absolutely nerveless under fire. Zeb had told him many times that that was what made the difference. With practice came the smooth motion and speed. But shooting at cans or bottles was one thing and plenty of men had failed to take into account the difference of facing another gun. That was where the nerves came into play. The lightning-fast practice draw might turn into a sweaty-handed, bungling motion with the mind shouting terror to frozen fingers. There was just no way of knowing until it actually happened. And Darby, watching the young man, could only wonder if there was something in Jory Parnes' past that made him falter on the draw. Whatever it was, Darby promised himself he would try to take Paxton out with his shotgun if the Hightower ramrod forced a showdown.

They rode into a small town in southeast Idaho called Downey. They'd been on the trail almost a week, and during that time Jory hadn't stopped practicing. But his lack of improvement was discouraging. Darby wasted no time in locating the gunsmith. He couldn't stand to watch the kid struggle with the Navy Colt.

Quinn's Gun Shop was businesslike; one entire wall was covered with wooden pegs upon which hung everything from buffalo rifles to dueling pistols. The room smelled of oil, leather, and gunpowder. Across from the entrance, Darby saw Quinn, a stiff, bent figure, with thick, wire-rimmed glasses and unruly gray hair. He wore a tie and a white shirt with the sleeves rolled up clear to his biceps. He nodded politely but didn't move, in a way that suggested he was more interested in his work than customers.

"Take a look-see around," he chirped. "My name is Quinn just like on the sign. Call me if you want to buy anything; otherwise close the door on your way out."

Independent old devil, Darby thought. He glanced back

at the wall of guns but, after a few minutes, lost interest and returned his attention to Quinn. The man was totally absorbed in filing some part of a weapon. Every few seconds, he raised it up to the window, eyed it critically, then attacked it again with vigor. After several minutes, Quinn stopped, reached for a nearby smoking pipe, crammed it into his mouth, and said, "You fellas got any money? Don't matter to me, but I don't let you fire anything until I see cash."

"I have money," Darby said stiffly. "And I'd prefer to look at a hot bath rather than your arsenal."

The gunsmith placed his pipe down, then climbed from his stool. "All right," he said, eying Darby's buckskins and making a decision. "You want a big huntin' rifle, I imagine. Well, I've got a beauty for sale. Almost new. It's a Sharps .45 caliber breech-loading single shot, plenty accurate enough to pop the eye out of a bear at six hundred yards. There's a lot of grizzly in these hills and skins are . . ."

Darby stopped him in midsentence. "I need a gunfighter's pistol and holster. Something light and fast."

The pale eyes behind the wire rims blinked. They traveled up and down Darby's length. The dirty buckskins, the unshaven face. "You're talking about quite a bit of money."

"That's of no concern. The only thing I care about," Darby said, "is that it's the best you've got."

"I see. So you're going to switch from hunting game to hunting man. That it?"

"No. The pistol isn't for me. It's for him," Darby said, gesturing toward Jory Parnes.

A smile. Here was someone with more promise. "Oh sure! Should have guessed it right away." A knowing, crafty look. "What's the matter, boy? Someone big shove you around and you're fixin' to even the score?"

"No," Jory said quickly.

Quinn waved as if to shoo away a fly. "No matter. Whatever your reasons, I got exactly what you want. A gun that'll make you nine feet tall no matter what company you're in.

THE GUN. Beautifully made, perfectly balanced—and revolutionary."

"What do you mean, 'revolutionary'?" Darby asked suddenly.

Quinn winked. "I'm just using the word that Smith & Wesson does. And from the moment I laid eyes on this gun, I knew they weren't exaggeratin' one damn bit."

"Let's see it," Darby said eagerly.

The old man hurried into the back room and returned cradling a small box. He placed it down on his workbench and carefully untied the string that bound it shut. Then, with a flourish, he swept off the lid and Darby leaned forward.

"So, after all these years, they've finally done it," he whispered. "Metallic cartridges!"

Darby reached into the box and picked up a cartridge between thumb and forefinger. "Amazing!" He showed it to Jory. "Beautiful and so deadly, isn't it? No more black powder flask, caps, or balls to drop and slow a man down. Just that, my friend, a neat, perfectly formed instrument of death."

Darby replaced the cartridge and picked up the gun, surprised by its lightness. As a writer, his research had included the standard frontier weapons, but this was a product that antiquated everything else on the market. "Tell me about it, Mr. Quinn."

He was only too happy to do so. "As you can see, it's Smith & Wesson. Always a quality manufacturer, yet I was amazed that they're the first out with it. As soon as Colt's patent on the revolving cylinder expired, they used it, together with the Rollin White patent for boring the cylinder all the way through so you can insert the new cartridges in the back, easy as can be."

"It's lighter, too," Darby said.

"You're right. They've cut down on some of the heavy metal across the top, shortened the barrel. But it'll stand up, I can tell by the balance she's well made. Uses a center-fire cartridge with twenty-five grains of powder and a two-hundred-eighteen-grain bullet. There isn't a gun on the market that will match it for quickness or accuracy. I fired it myself 'cause I couldn't keep my hands off of it."

He chuckled. "Yes, sir, Smith & Wesson has outdone Colt and Remington both. There ain't a finer .44 caliber in the world. So, if the kid needs the best, you're alookin' at it in your hand, mister."

Darby nodded his head in strong agreement. The gun *was* revolutionary. With practice, a man could probably reload at least four or five times faster than with the standard cap-and-ball weapons men used. The cartridge also had the major advantage of being a self-contained unit. The powder charge would always be exactly the same, calculated to project the bullet a certain distance at a predetermined velocity. Gone would be the problems of varying qualities of black powder, and caps and balls of fractionally different sizes that were a constant worry to men whose lives often rested squarely on the dependability of their weapons. A remarkable break-through! Long overdue, he had no doubt that the cartridge would replace black powder pistols and rifles in a very few years. Smith & Wesson had clearly outmaneuvered both Colt and Remington as an innovator.

"Well," Quinn said, "what do you say? I've ordered more, but the company can't keep up with everyone's demand so I ain't selling it cheap."

"Do you have a large supply of cartridges? This gun is useless if we can't find enough ammunition out here."

"How much do you want?" Quinn asked.

"A thousand rounds."

"I've got only eight hundred."

Darby passed the gun to Jory, noticed how the kid's hand trembled. "I think I ought to buy it, if you're agreeable."

Jory's fingers tightened over the smooth gun butt. He turned the weapon, first one way, then the other. When he spoke, his voice was husky. "It's . . . it's too fine a weapon for the likes of me. I can't let you buy it."

Darby placed a hand on Jory's shoulder. "You saved my life. It's a small repayment and I'm trying to save yours. Please, take it."

Jory drew himself up tall. "I guess I will, then. Thanks."

"Good! Does it come with a holster?" Darby asked, turning back to Quinn.

"No. But I made one for it. A gunfighter's holster! Fit to hold that pistol, then let it go fast."

"Then we'll want it, too. Let's see him try it out."

As soon as Jory belted the holster on, Darby realized there was a risk involved that he hadn't considered. With the Smith & Wesson resting in a cut-down holster tied to his leg, Jory looked like a kid out to build a gunfighter's reputation. But that wasn't, and never would be, the case. And Jory wasn't fast, not yet anyway. The trouble was that he didn't have much time to learn how to draw before they crossed tracks with Paxton Bullock. Perhaps this gun, this perfect instrument of destruction he now held in his fist, would even the odds—at least give Jory a chance.

The gun hung out from his hips, but Jory didn't seem to care. His eyes were more alive than Darby had seen them yet, and he felt a chill pass through his body as he waited for Jory to draw. How much difference *would* this gun make?

Jory's fingers splayed out over the gun butt. He swiveled around to face the wall; his back stiffened. Suddenly, he made his draw. Darby heard flesh strike the grips and watched the Smith & Wesson come up. Then Jory dropped it, clattering, to the floor. Instantly, he scooped it up, his face pale.

Jory's shoulders sagged. He held the gun up before his eyes as if to ask it—why? The gunsmith walked back to his workbench and found he'd not quite filed the piece of metal the way he wanted it. The room was silent.

"Try it again," Darby whispered. "It's new. No matter what he told you, that gun isn't going to make you good overnight, Jory. You've got to practice until your arms ache and then practice some more."

Jory shook his head sadly, defeat showing in every muscle in his face. "It's time I told you."

"Told me what?"

Jory slipped the pistol back into the holster and started to unbuckle it. His eyes were downcast. "I never will be any good with a gun," he whispered. "About three years ago, I roped a mustang and caught three fingers in my dally. Almost lost them but some of the boys sewed them up with hair from the mane of my horse."

Jory held up his hand. "You can hardly see the scars. Them boys did a good job. But the fingers are mostly numb to the tips. That's one reason I never even tried to learn the draw before now. I can get the gun out but when I start fixin' to pull back the hammer and trigger . . ." His voice trailed off. He unbuckled the cartridge belt, held it out to Darby.

"Have you been to a doctor?" Darby asked.

"What for?" Jory replied. "The feeling is gone and I'm lucky to have fingers. Besides, I can handle a rope, hold things just fine. Up until this trouble, I never really worried about it much. I knew I'd have trouble with the caps and reloading. Rolling a cigarette became a big joke for the boys, so I gave it up entirely."

Darby scowled. "What about your other hand. You could draw with it, couldn't you?"

"It's my left hand!"

"It's also your sound one. Why don't you try?"

Jory didn't look a bit receptive to the idea. "Look," he argued, "you're a writer. Can you write left-handed?"

"I'd learn," Darby said flatly, "if there was no choice."

He turned to the gunsmith. "Do you have any left-handed holsters?"

The old man chewed his pipe for a moment before speaking. "It's none of my business, but I think he'd be a lot better off buying a Winchester rifle than trying to learn how to draw with the wrong paw. It just wouldn't work. He'd never be any good. Let me show you this rifle over here. Doesn't cost any more than . . ."

"Wait a minute!" Something he'd read came to Darby's mind. He strode over and picked up the gun, eyed down its barrel, and brushed by the gunsmith. Before the old man could protest, he snatched up the file and started rasping the sight off. It wasn't much of a job, no more than a bead.

"Hey! What are you doin'! That sight ain't big enough to catch in a holster."

"Maybe not a holster," Darby grunted. "How much do I owe you?"

"Fifty-two dollars. But I'll throw in a holster cheap."

Darby paid him then and left with the pistol in his hand and Jory hurrying to catch up.

"What did you do that for? Where are we going?"

"To get a hotel room and a bath," Darby said. "Then I'm going to show you how to stay alive."

It was midmorning when they stopped and Darby wasted no time. "Go ahead and start practicing as I showed you."

Jory nodded, stuck the gun under his belt. They'd worked on it hard the night before but hadn't accomplished much beyond positioning the gun. With his long arms and fingers, he had good reach. The pistol would go in front of his right hipbone, the butt turned slightly outward.

Darby eyed it critically. "That's right," he said, "just like Bill Eastman wore it."

Jory shook his head forlornly. "But you told me you'd read that Eastman died in a shoot-out. It must not have worked."

"It *did* work. Mr. Eastman outdrew a number of gunfighters this way. The only reason he died, I think, is because he got drunk in a barroom and tried to draw. He simply forgot to step back far enough from the rail."

"All right," Jory said, "but I wish you were a little surer of the facts."

Darby lit a cigar and squinted through blue smoke. "What we're banking on is the element of surprise. Paxton will be watching your right hand. He'll have no idea you'll draw with your left. In that position, the weapon could be pulled either way but he knows you're right-handed. That will give you a split-second advantage and you'll have to make the most of it."

"It'll only work once," Jory said. "I'd never get away with it a second time."

"I think," Darby said slowly, "that should be the least of your worries. Now, start by just getting the gun out smoothly. Don't rush. Each time we stop, we'll speed up the motion a fraction of a second. In three days, you'll be drawing as fast as you can."

"I'm afraid that won't be very fast. But I'll try."

He did, too. The first day, Darby forced him to go slowly because he knew it would be discouraging. And it was. Jory tried not to show his feelings but, even for a nineteen-year-old, switching from right to left wasn't easy. Jory said he felt he was off balance and fighting his whole body every time he made a grab for the weapon. His right hand always jumped forward and finally Darby had him jam it into his pocket. Later that evening, young Jory wasn't interested in trying to write. He just rolled up in his blankets and went to sleep.

Darby fed the campfire late that night and his mind was troubled. For the first time in many months, he drank an entire bottle of brandy, but it didn't help. He needed Jory Parnes to show him about mustanging and he genuinely liked the young man's company. But neither factor was worth the danger of Jory facing Paxton Bullock in a lop-sided gun duel. Darby hoped that such a mismatch would never take place and he swore to the burning embers that he would prevent it from happening. He'd stay close to the kid when they were in town and he'd carry the sawed-off shotgun at all times. Yet, there were always unexpected things.

And if Paxton killed *him*, Jory would be on his own without much chance.

A soft night wind rustled in the trees and the brandy finally took effect. Hunkered down by his cold fire, Darby drifted off to sleep. Dressed in his buckskins with a beard already covering his face, he appeared to be anything but what he really was—an Easterner, a dime novelist, a man who'd drunk too much brandy and was genuinely troubled about what lay ahead for a boy who might have been like his own son.

The next day they passed through rugged hills and the country became dry. On a barren ridge covered with stunted chaparral and rabbit brush, they gazed south to the Great Salt Lake. From a distance, the water looked fresh and blue, promising instant refreshment to the weary traveler. But it was deceiving; Darby could smell that water and see the stunted trees on the hillsides and the parched, cracked mud flats glistening white in the sunlight. Resting at the fringes of great arid spaces, he found the lake a mockery and a waste. They pushed on to the west, stopping every few hours to rest the horses, and to test Jory and the gun.

That second day, the practice went better. Despite his stated intentions, Darby let him draw as fast as he could. But it seemed the harder Jory tried, the worse it became. In desperation, Darby had him target-shoot with his left hand, and for the first time in two days, there was a glimmer of hope. Jory was amazed to find that he could unload the gun into a small piñon pine at fifty feet with rare misses by firing from hip level. He could do no better with his right hand. And, true to promise, the Smith & Wesson was perfectly balanced and operated with almost a life of its own. Jory was so encouraged he wrote his first complete sentence that night: "I like my new pistull. Thank you, Jory Parnes."

Just before he fell asleep, Jory said, "I think I can get to be accurate with this. If Paxton misses or doesn't put me down with his first bullet, I'll get him." There was a pause.

"But, Darby, I won't ever be any good on the draw with my left hand. I want you to know that; it could save your life."

Darby rolled over in his blankets. "You're wrong," he said angrily, "you haven't given it any time. And if you've convinced yourself it's hopeless, it will be."

"There isn't *enough* time!" Jory snapped. "Maybe if I had a year . . . maybe I could get fast, but I doubt it. We'll be in Elko by the end of this week."

"Yes, thank God. But remember, Paxton is just starting back from Cheyenne. You've got time. Keep trying. You're a lot faster than you give yourself credit for."

Jory sighed. "I wish I could believe that."

Four nights later, camped near a thick stand of juniper, it happened. They were gathering firewood and Darby had just reached down for a branch when he heard the chilling sound of a rattler. He was in a bad position. Half-stooped with one arm full, the wood dropped as he froze. The snake was coiled under a bush. He saw its fangs, the pointing red tongue. It would strike and there was no way he could avoid getting bitten.

Jory's head snapped around as Darby's armload of wood fell. In a split second, he saw the rattler and at the same instant he streaked for his gun. It *was* the same motion he'd made a thousand times since Quinn's Gun Shop, but it *wasn't*. It was an unthinking act, a well-conditioned reflex he never knew he had. The .44 came from his waist in a fluid blur, the kind of movement that only happens when the muscles are trained to react faster than thought. His first bullet split snakeskin on the soft, creamy underbelly and flipped the rattler sideways. The second and third shots punctured the sides and the fourth slug blew off its head.

Darby straightened. He could feel the sweat jumping from every pore on his body. Across the distance, their eyes met, and slowly, their mouths formed smiles.

Jory stared at the smoking gun in his hand as though he'd

never seen it before. And maybe, in a way, he hadn't, Darby reflected. "Thank you."

"Don't mention it," the kid replied. "Reckon we've got enough wood. If you start the fire, I'll hunt us up a cotton-tail for dinner."

Darby picked up his fallen armload of wood. "The Winchester?"

"I don't think I'll be needing it," Jory said, reloading.

"No, I don't believe you will." Darby started back to camp. After dried beef, rabbit was going to taste wonderful.

CHAPTER 6

In the northeast corner of Nevada, rising out of the vast, arid plateaus, stand the Ruby Mountains. They are not of majestic proportions like the Colorado Rockies, nor tall and proud like the Sierra Nevada, but Darby Buckingham found them to his liking. He learned from Jory that Nevada mountains washboard the state north to south, and are generally worn, tired, and brown. But the gentle Rubys are cool and verdant, a place where snows remain almost until summer and streams dash from the rocky slopes into waiting valleys. These valleys swallow the water and yield tall grasses while, less than a day's ride away, tough desert chaparral fights to survive on land blasted by sun burning through high desert air.

It is a place of striking contrasts created by the presence or absence of water. And though Darby was no cattleman, his eyes looked down to the Ruby-fed Humboldt River and he smiled. They reined their horses to a standstill at the mountain's base and dismounted.

"This is Hightower's range?" he asked.

"Not all of it," Jory replied. "Even Hench has his limitations. See those mountains way out there toward the northwest?"

They were brown, like a row of fallen, rotting logs. He judged them to be almost fifty miles away. "Yes."

"They're called the Independence Mountains. Just beyond them are the Tuscaroras. And in between is a valley running north and south for at least a hundred miles. That's Paxton's hunting ground. It's tough country, not nearly as green as here. Instead of fir, pine, and aspen in the canyons, it's mostly juniper and piñon. But it's the finest wild-horse country I've ever seen."

Darby nodded. In the cool Rubys, he gazed out toward a hostile and inferior environment. Though it was only May, he could almost see the heat shimmering from the Independence Range.

Maybe Jory read his mind because he said, "Hightower has a crew working in these mountains, too. But I'm not sure where. There's a good chance we could stay up here and have the whole summer go by without meeting anyone. There's enough mustangs in these Rubys to last us years."

Darby glanced around to the young man beside him. "Where's Hightower's main ranch?"

Jory pointed north. "It's a hard ride up from Elko, nearly to Mason Peak at the headwaters of Beaver Creek. Like every other ranch in this country, it's near good water and in a deep valley. Hench built his house and outbuildings right against the base of a low mountain overlooking his valley."

"Then," Darby said slowly, "Paxton works just east of there, near those Tuscaroras you spoke about?"

"That's right."

"Well, I'd say if we came to put the man out of the mustanging business or at least to make him change his ways, we'd better ride north for those Independence Mountains."

Jory chuckled. "You're set on going right after him, aren't you?"

Darby pulled a Cuban cigar out of his saddlebag, bit off the tip, and lit it. He inhaled deeply and expelled the smoke with almost a sigh. "You've got the picture, my young friend. Frankly, I'm not interested in capturing the mustangs at all. But those that we do catch will be well treated and we'll keep only the ones that will make good saddle horses."

"And the rest?"

"We'll drive them off Mr. Hightower's range."

"He's not going to let us get away with that, Darby. I sure

hope you've got a plan or we won't be around the next time
snow falls on this mountain. We're going to need a lot of
help."

The easterner smiled. "You're worried, aren't you?"

"Damn right," Jory blurted. "You saw Paxton and know
what he'll do when he finds us camped on his stompin'
grounds. And . . . and I wish you wouldn't smile like that!"

Jory continued to practice drawing his gun. It was a habit
now. Every time he had a few free moments, he was pulling
out the Smith & Wesson as naturally as a dog scratching at
his fleas. Since killing the rattler, he'd gained enough confidence to mark a steady improvement. He probably wasn't as
fast as Paxton and perhaps never would be, but Darby still
hoped he might beat their enemy with his surprise edge.

"And furthermore," Jory was telling him, "I don't see how
moving poor horses off this range will do anything. Like I
told you back in Running Springs, they'll come hightailing it
back."

Darby scowled and lapsed into brooding silence. He
wasn't sure what they'd accomplish besides making big trouble. But he couldn't shake the memory of Hightower's cruelty and he never would. And now, as he sat smoking the
Cuban and gazing across the valley toward distant peaks
and the Hightower land, he realized he wanted trouble.
He wanted to strike back at the rancher any way he could
within the law. The only way he could do that, it seemed,
was to break Hightower's domination in this raw country.
Break it and then hope that those who took his place were
men like Jory Parnes. He knew that this was the best he
could accomplish, even with luck. In the back of his mind, if
he survived what lay ahead, he thought it might be worth-
while to travel to Carson City and petition an end to sense-
lessly killing wild horses.

"Darby?"

"Yeah."

"How many men are you thinking of hiring besides me?"

Darby shrugged his heavy shoulders. "You're the mustanger. You tell me."

"We need at least half a dozen men with experience." Jory's mouth crimped. "It would also help if they were handy with guns."

"I don't want to start a range war, just catch horses."

"No one is going to go up against Hightower unless he's well paid. It could wind up costing you a lot of money. Maybe even sixty dollars a man."

Darby finished his cigar. It was time to leave. "Then that's what I'll advertise at," he said, leading the gelding to a fallen log.

"I know of a few good men who *might* be interested," Jory said.

"Then look them up when we reach town, my friend, because I don't plan to spend all summer out there in the hills. It's my intention to have this thing settled and over before the weather becomes hot. I want to spend those days near a cool stream with a glass of good brandy in my left hand and a quill in my right. The New York Publishing House is generous with me, but they do expect another exciting Western saga from this experience."

"You mean," Jory's eyes widened, "you mean you're going to write this all up in a book?"

"I do."

"And will I be in it?"

"Oh," Darby said, angling for an outburst, "I hadn't thought much about it." That was a lie. He'd already decided that Jory Parnes would make a perfect hero—if they survived.

Jory couldn't mask the excitement in his voice. "I'd like to be," he said quickly, "no matter how it ends, I sure would be proud to be in your story."

Darby found a rock and mounted. "Well," he said, appearing to weigh the question with great care, "on one condition."

"Anything!"

"You'll have to be able to read the whole book when it's published."

"You got a deal."

"Good," Darby said with an enthusiastic nod. "Now let's get down to Elko. There's a lot of work to do."

Darby Buckingham had to buy a pair of suspenders to keep his pants from sliding to the floor. In his hotel room, he surveyed himself in the mirror. Yes, the white shirt and black coat still fit perfectly. But the full beard gave him a rather wild appearance and his pants were at least three inches too big at the waist. That concerned him somewhat, because Buckinghams were, by their nature, robust. To Darby, a little extra fat was a good thing and showed that he was a gentleman of leisure and a connoisseur of fine food and drink. But, in Elko, he suspected that he wouldn't be staying long enough to experience any leisure and he'd be greatly surprised if the town offered much in the way of exciting cuisine.

His trunks had preceded him to the hotel, and freshly bathed, he strode back and forth, just experiencing the luxury of being clothed in good fabric rather than animal skin. Even his derby hat felt good and had survived the journey without being crumpled. Darby poked two cigars into his coat pocket and headed for the newspaper office.

The editor, a Mr. Plankton, greeted him warmly when Darby stated he sought advertising. But when it became clear what Darby's intentions were, Mr. Plankton's expression grew quite serious.

"Mr. Buckingham," he said, "I'll run notices for you to be distributed all over town. And I'll place advertising in this Sunday's papers."

Darby waited. There was more and he could guess it would be a warning. When Plankton continued, Darby's suspicion was correct.

"But I must warn you, sir. I take no responsibility for the consequences. Furthermore, I feel obligated to say that the

advertisement, as you've worded it, will bring an immediate
and unpleasant reaction from Hench Hightower."

"Then," Darby replied, "it will have served its purpose.
As far as the wording is concerned, I see nothing wrong
with being honest in my intention to run Mr. Hightower out
of business unless he agrees to amend his cruel practices.
Now, when will my advertising see print?"

"Tomorrow. I'll set the type this afternoon and I've got a
few kids who will tack up your notices first thing in the
morning."

The editor was a pleasant enough man; Darby judged him
to be in his early thirties, surely married, with children. He
had that settled look of a man who is both competent and
content with his station in life.

"I wouldn't," Darby said, "want to cause you trouble with
Mr. Hightower. Yet, I do need your services."

Plankton smiled, removed his glasses, and wiped them on
his shirt before replacing them. "Don't worry about me. I
know how Hench operates and I've never had anything
good to say about the man since I bought this paper three
years ago. Besides, he's going to be so furious at you that you
won't even think about it being my paper. I'm a businessman
and you've got money to pay. Also, I plan to follow your
story rather closely. It will be a welcome addition to church
affairs and barroom brawls." Plankton gazed fondly at his
printing press. "You're going to provide a great deal of interest for my readers—if you aren't shot right away."

Darby swallowed dryly; Plankton wasn't a man who dealt
in subtleties. "Just take care of the advertising, I'll take care
of myself," he said stiffly.

"I'll do that. But, if you don't mind, I'd like to make one
suggestion. It's that you wait a few days. In a town this
small, I know pretty much the way people move and Hightower will be riding in the day our newspaper comes out.
You might be better off to sit quiet until he leaves. Then, by
the time he comes back, you'd at least have a start and some
men to back your gamble."

It was probably excellent advice and Darby knew the newspaper editor meant well. But there was an element of sneakiness in the suggestion he didn't like. What Plankton suggested was that he lock himself up in his room and hide until the powerful rancher left. He couldn't do that. Besides, there was always an outside chance he and Hightower could sit down over a bottle of whiskey and reach some kind of agreement. But Darby didn't expect that to happen. It would be too easy and, from the rancher's point of view, unnecessary.

"Thanks anyway, sir. But I have a feeling everyone in Elko would realize the basis for the delay and that would create doubt in their minds as to whether I mean to do as I say."

Plankton shrugged. "There'll be plenty of doubt anyway. But most of it will be whether or not you survive the day. If Paxton Bullock were back, I'd have suggested you ride a fast horse out of town right now. But don't let his absence fool you—Hench has a few more almost as mean. And they're always trying to outdo one another in Hench's eyes. He pays his ramrods gunfighter's wages because that's exactly what they are."

Darby nodded and stepped outside. Tomorrow was Saturday and his fliers would go out in the morning. With luck, he might be able to hire a crew and make a show of force by the time Hightower and friends hit Elko. But Plankton's warning did have him worried. That's why, at the last minute, he'd raised the advertised wages to seventy-five dollars a month and found. Damn, he thought, he'd better get to writing. It would take a fair chunk of his royalties just to float this mustang adventure. Still, it would be money well spent. His readers would get a satisfying Western story based on his own firsthand knowledge, and the mustangs also would benefit.

Darby started toward the Stockman's Saloon. In twenty-four hours, the word would be all over town and, at the wages he was paying, he'd have his crew. In forty-eight hours, the showdown with Hightower would be over—one way or another. But right now, he intended to find the biggest steak in Elko, and the most refined bottle of wine the town could offer.

On Saturday, ten men and a girl sought him out for the job. Three of them were drunks and one was a crazy old man who spit chewing tobacco all over his shirt whenever he talked. He'd introduced himself as Jerome Jerome, and when he said it, he streaked Darby's shirt so badly he knew he'd never be able to get the tobacco stains out.

Jerome Jerome might have been sixty, but if so, he'd lived them far harder than anyone should. He cupped his hand behind his right ear whenever Darby spoke and answered with a roar to set the dogs barking up and down Elko's back streets. He was in terrible shape—over forty years as a bronc buster, town tamer, and womanizer. Darby glanced over at Jory to see his reaction, but the kid wasn't smiling. In fact, there was intense interest on his face. But his answer to Jerome Jerome was still the same and the tall tobacco spitter ambled out of the room with his back straight as a rod.

"You should have hired him," Jory said. "I'm surprised he even showed up."

"So am I," Darby clipped. "I'm wondering how he got up the hotel steps."

"He's good," Jory insisted. "Almost a legend."

"Look. I didn't insult him, did I?"

"If you had, you'd have a knife in your ribs by now," Jory said, "but I told him you were a dude who didn't mean anything but good for the horses. That's why he came."

Darby was incredulous. "You mean *he's* one of those men you were going to talk to?"

"The first," Jory said flatly. "That old man taught me how to fork a bronc. He was the best."

"'Was' is right. But if I ever saw living proof that bronc riding is hard on a man's body, he's it. What's wrong with his hearing?"

"He's just lit on his head a few times. That's all."

"He doesn't walk too well either."

"Don't need to, Darby. Jerome Jerome spends all his wakin' hours in a saddle."

He dabbed at his starched white shirt with a handkerchief. The tobacco juice was already soaked in. "I imagine the front of his horse is the color of a walking spittoon," Darby grumbled.

But at least he had a crew. And maybe when the newspaper itself came out, others would step forward. Plankton had assured him the paper would be picked up on the stage and be read in other towns. Darby asked the editor to send anyone out who looked especially good. Besides Jerome Jerome, a sassy young tomboy named Maggie Lamesa, and the three drunks, he had six men who appeared to know their business.

Of all the interviews, the one with the girl had been the most difficult. Magdalena Lamesa was probably seventeen going on thirty. She had short black hair and brown eyes that Darby had found to be rather beautiful. When she'd first entered the room, Jory had stiffened.

"So you finally got fed up with crippling mustangs for Hench, did you?" she said flatly.

"Maggie, you know I never . . ."

"Aw, shut up, Jory. I didn't come up here to talk to you." Her eyes raked up and down Darby. "Jory, did you tell this dude about Hench and what's going to happen tomorrow?"

"This dude," Jory said hotly, "whipped Paxton Bullock two weeks ago. He knows exactly what he's up against. 'Sides that—" Jory hesitated to heighten the impact, "'sides that, Mr. Buckingham is a great writer who is doing a book on mustanging and I'm going to be in black and white right on the pages."

Miss Lamesa's eyes lost their frostiness and she walked up closer to Darby as if to make sure she was seeing correctly. She pointed at him questioningly. "*You* whipped Paxton?"

"Well," Darby said with a shrug, "he really isn't a skilled pugilist."

"A what?" Her nose wrinkled with the question.

"A fighter, I meant to say," Darby explained, "although he is quite good with his boots."

"Yeah," Jory added, "I still feel it in my ribs."

"So," she said, "he finally got around to kicking you. What for?"

"'Cause I busted him on the jaw. I got in the first lick."

Maggie Lamesa said what Darby guessed was her highest form of a compliment. "He'll kill you both for sure, but you got a right to be proud."

"Well, thanks," Jory mumbled. "That's about the first nice thing you ever said to me."

"Well, don't go giddy over it." She was back to form now, and dressed in her dusty riding clothes, she looked all business. "I'm interested in working for anyone who works against Hightower. I can ride and rope and shoot a whole lot straighter than Jory. Isn't that right?"

"Yeah, yeah, sure," Jory said, blushing. "She's a hand for sure."

She strode up to Darby. "How about it?"

He reached for a cigar, playing for time. She was a fighter and probably better than most of the men he'd hired. But she was so young and . . . and small. She was a girl! A girl in a boy's pants and shirt. She couldn't have weighed much over a hundred pounds. She was all spit and fight and . . . he couldn't hire her. The thought of someone as young as Jory facing Hightower's guns was enough to leave him sleepless. But to drag in a girl no more than seventeen was too much for Darby's conscience.

He lit his cigar, desperately trying to come up with some gentle way of saying no. He needn't have bothered. She looked down at the floor, closed her eyes for a moment, then whispered, "The hell with you, mister. You are a fool."

Before Darby could stop her, Maggie Lamesa was gone.

"Blast!" Darby swore. He glared at Jory and the young man shifted uneasily.

"Don't blame me. I'd have hired her."

"A girl?"

"Yeah! A girl who'll work harder than most any cowboy we've signed on yet."

"You're the one who told me women were trouble. I don't need the worry of protecting the honor of Miss Lamesa," Darby said hotly. "In case you didn't notice—and maybe she hasn't either—that girl is very . . ."

"She's good lookin', ain't she?" Jory said, smiling.

"Yes, yes, she is."

"Well, I noticed it a couple of years ago. She almost shot me off my horse. You're wrong about needing to protect her honor. That girl is her own best protection."

Darby didn't need convincing.

Jory walked over to the window and looked down into the street. "There she goes," he said quietly.

After a moment, he turned around. "Nobody can prove anything, but her dad was a mustanger who figured there were enough wild horses for more than one rancher. He was good, too." A sharpness slid into Jory's tone. "One day, he got drug to death by his stirrup."

"An accident?"

"Yeah." Jory's face clouded. "There's no proof, but some people think the accident was running up against Hench Hightower."

"I see. Did anyone ever ask Hench?"

Jory laughed, but it wasn't a pleasant sound. "Maggie did. Right out there in the street with the entire town watching. Hench just laughed in her face. But I've heard folks say that, if she wasn't a girl, she'd be dead."

"What about the sheriff in this town?"

"Forget about him. John Salton isn't on anyone's payroll, but he's no fool either. I'd say when they found Maggie's father, John was mighty happy to call it an accident. Most everything is an accident as far as Salton is concerned."

"So I've heard," Darby grumbled. "Paxton told me about that."

"It's worth remembering."

Darby consulted his watch. It was almost time for dinner and he needed a drink. "Jory, go find the six men we hired. Is there a quiet saloon in this town?"

"The Waterhole Bar is probably the tamest. Why?"

"Tell them to come by in about an hour and we'll make our plans. Tomorrow is Sunday and I want to be on our way by the next afternoon."

"Sounds good, boss. The sooner we get started, the better."

Darby sat at a rear table sipping beer. The Waterhole Bar wasn't much. It was long, narrow, and dark. There was a boarded-over set of windows facing the street. Maybe too many cowboys had been thrown through them to make it worth-while replacing the glass every time a fight ended. Whatever the reason, the only light was from the open front door and that didn't reach very far into the interior.

He was nursing his third beer and it was past six o'clock by his watch. His thoughts were unpleasant. He was sick of hearing about Hightower and feeling more than a little unhappy about the way he'd had to turn Maggie Lamesa away. But the six he had hired looked like veterans who could take care of themselves. They would have to be.

"Hey, mister!"

Darby glanced up. A man he didn't know stood by the door. He was out of breath and flushed with excitement. Darby jumped up from his table, knowing something was wrong.

"You better git over to the Stockman's, 'cause Parnes and those other fools you hired are gettin' kicked all over the saloon by Hightower's boys. It's no contest at all! And . . ."

Darby didn't wait to hear the rest of it. He was up and moving. Outside, he ran down the boardwalk. He stopped only once and that was to yank a Winchester rifle out of someone's saddle boot. Hench Hightower had come calling.

CHAPTER 7

He was too late. Slamming his shoulder into the batwing doors, he charged into the saloon to find a roisterous crowd of Hightower wranglers lined up at the bar. They were laughing and pounding each other on the back—until he raised the Winchester and fired. Everyone froze.

"Darby!"

He spun around, trying to locate Jory's voice. Then he saw them, back near the far wall. Jory was sitting at a poker table with a man who could only be Hench Hightower. Standing behind Hench were two men he instantly sized up as Paxton Bullock types, only without the beef. They drifted toward him, their faces expressionless.

Darby went to meet them. Out of the corner of his eye, he saw three men lying on the floor. He stopped and made sure. Yes, they were ones he'd hired just yesterday and they were beaten almost senseless. He didn't need to ask anyone why. And, when he turned back toward the poker table, he saw a handsome man of perhaps sixty with a look on his face that was both smug and contemptuous. Something exploded inside Darby Buckingham.

Without breaking stride, he continued on, knowing the two bodyguards weren't going to let him close to their boss. They circled in on him just as he knew they would. When they were close, Darby switched his grip on the rifle and brought it up, butt first and hard. It cracked against the first man's jaw. Darby pivoted and rammed the barrel into the other's stomach as hard as he could, bringing him down to stay.

The movement was so fast, the second man's gasp erupted

before his friend hit the floor. Two more strides and he grabbed Hench Hightower by the shirt and lifted him right out of his chair. Then he swung him up against the wall with enough force to shake the lamps on the ceiling. Before anyone could move, he yanked the rancher around and hooked his elbow across Hench's throat and lifted him off the floor.

"Anyone moves and I'll break this man's neck!"

For what seemed like a long time, there was no movement. Nothing, except the rasping of air in and out of Hightower's mouth. And though Darby couldn't see his face, he guessed the smugness was gone. "Tell all your crew to leave," Darby hissed, "you and I are going to have a talk."

Darby eased the pressure and carefully let the rancher down. Hightower wasn't very big. Maybe a hundred and forty pounds and well under six feet. As mad as Darby was, he realized he'd come very close to snapping the man's neck. As mad as he was, he didn't care.

Just for good measure, he jerked the rancher up tight again until his toes were almost off the ground. "Tell them!"

"Take it easy!" Jory cried. "He's choking to death!" Then, in a voice much lower, "If you kill him, we're finished."

It made sense, so Darby gave Hightower just enough air to speak. "Get . . . get out of here!"

The two bodyguards had to be carried out the front door and Darby waited until the saloon was empty before he relaxed his arm lock. When he did, he shoved Hightower into a chair.

"Keep him covered," Darby ordered. He strode over to the bar and grabbed a bottle of whiskey. Seconds later, he was pouring it down the throats of his hired hands, coaxing them back to sensibility. None of them were badly hurt. He made sure of that. But when he finally got them to their feet, there was something in their eyes he hadn't seen the day before—fear.

Shorty Callister seemed to be the one with a mind to speak and his words were brutally frank. "You've done it now," he said through puffy lips, "that old man is going to have both of your hides."

"Uh-uh," Darby grunted, "he and I will reach an understanding before we part. We're holding the gun, not him."

"Bull!" Hightower snarled, "you kill me and my boys will burn this place down if they have to. No one will get out alive."

Darby twisted around to stare at the rancher. What he saw was anything but fright. The old man glared at him redly and Darby knew he wasn't bluffing one damn bit. If Hightower had been a younger man, Darby would have taken great pleasure in physically punishing him. But he wasn't young, only old and mean and gutsy. It posed a real problem.

"We're leavin'," Shorty said.

Darby turned back to what was left of his crew. He needed to change their minds but Shorty didn't give him a chance.

"We gave a good account of ourselves. Jory fought like a crazy man and it took two of his boys to wrassle me down long enough to knock me out. We got nothin' to be ashamed of, Buckingham."

"Of course you don't! That's why I . . ."

"So it's not like we was running or nothing," Shorty said, pushing on. "But you can't beat the odds, even if you're rich enough to hire forty or fifty hard cases like he's got."

"He's smarter than he looks," Hightower said caustically, "you'd better take his advice."

"Shut up!" Darby raged. Old or not, if the rancher interrupted again, he meant to make him eat his teeth.

"Listen, Shorty. All three of you. If it takes hiring a crew as big and rough as he's got, then I'll do that," Darby said. "What is going on here is wrong and we all know it. If you stay on my payroll, we'll find enough others to insure this never happens again."

Shorty Callister shook his head. "You're dreamin', mister. The only reason you got the six of us was that we was new

to this country and didn't know the deck was stacked. We
was passing through and saw your posters all over town.
Should have had enough sense to guess that you wouldn't
pay those kind of wages unless there was a big hitch in the
deal."

He reached into his mouth and pulled out a loose tooth.
He hurled it to the floor and spat blood. "Taking a beating
is one thing; taking a bullet, like you're setting us up for, is
entirely different."

Darby knew he was wasting his breath. He saw the same
haunted, fearful look in all their faces. Maybe they were just
smart. "All right," he sighed.

Shorty glanced up quickly, then back down to the floor.
"Good luck. You'll need it. Hey, bartender, is that the back
door?"

"Yeah, straight into the alley."

"Much obliged." He pointed to the whiskey bottle.
"You'd better drink up, friend. This town ain't healthy."

Darby looked away until he heard the back door close. He
couldn't blame them. Shorty and the others were cowboys,
not gunfighters. They were wise enough to realize there was
a big difference.

"Jory, I don't know what happened between you and Paxton, but you're back on my payroll," Hightower said. "There
will be some hard feelings over this and you'll probably
have to stay at headquarters for a few months until everything simmers down. But you're a kid and this is the first
time you've ever stepped out of line. I'm willing to let this
one pass."

"Paxton isn't," Jory whispered. He looked confused,
whipped.

"He works for me!" Hightower rasped. "If I tell him to let
you alone, by God, he'll do it or he's finished in Nevada!"

Jory shook his head as if to dispel a fog. "I don't think you
know him as well as I do, Mr. Hightower. I don't think you
could fire Paxton."

The rancher started to protest, but for reasons Darby

couldn't fathom, whatever he was about to say, he held back. Instead, he slumped down in his chair. "Look, Jory. Paxton Bullock is my man and he takes orders only from me. I don't know why I'm telling you this, but I like your style. You're the best bronc twister I've ever seen and you'll get better. I'd like to have you back on the payroll because you are good at your job."

"Thanks," Jory said.

Darby strolled over to the bar and poured a whiskey. He also needed Jory but for different reasons. Yet, the young man had to make up his own mind.

"Paxton is also good," Hightower drawled, "very good at keeping control of my interests. But he's better at busting men than horses. Now listen, Jory. There's a notch for Paxton just as there's a notch for you in my plans. Maybe . . . maybe I've made a mistake putting you under him these past few years. But I'm a damn sharp judge of character and I thought you were a little soft."

"Soft?"

"Now, don't get mad, son."

Darby heard the response clearly. "I'm not your son, Mr. Hightower!"

"Take it easy, Jory. It's time you started thinking about yourself. You've got a man's decision to make and you'll never have a better chance than the one I'm offering now. I'm not sure what Buckingham promised, but if you walk out with me, I'll see you're running your own crew of mustangers this fall."

Jory's head turned and Darby saw he was struggling. Picking up his drink, he walked back and said, "Jory, he's right about one thing. It's your decision. Take his offer and I'm not going to blame you at all. But know this. He won't change the way things are and he'll go on killing and crippling horses as long as it pays to sell their hides."

"Mr. Hightower," Jory said urgently, "we don't need to shoot the stallions and . . . and I think we should just take the horses we can sell for mounts. Let the others be." Jory was pleading now. Desperate. His words were received in stony silence. "Mr. Hightower, there's too many good animals out there being ruined and . . ."

The rancher smiled in a pitying way that made Darby wish he'd broken his neck. "Jory, Jory. You don't understand. I'm a cattleman. You know that. Those mustangs are eating grass, wasting cattle feed. By midsummer when the water holes shrivel down to pothole size and the creeks go dry, those goddamn horses drink first and my cows die of thirst. And those thieving studs run off my mares and that's also costing me money."

"But . . ."

"Let me put it this way," Hightower said, tipping back in his chair and hooking his thumbs in his vest pocket, "I'm a businessman and mustangs are profitable, just like cattle. But if I go soft and let them multiply over my ranges, they become a huge liability and compete with my herds. As far as I'm concerned, they're no different than any other predator in that respect. It's them or me—a case of survival."

The chair tipped forward and Hightower said softly, "You're still half kid, Jory. And you're making a big mistake by mixing sentimentality with business. You've got a hell of a lot of growing up to do."

"Thanks, Mr. Hightower." Jory stood up quickly. "I appreciate the lecture and I've learned plenty by listening. And it's clear the reason why you want me to stay. Only you didn't quite say it all. You forgot to mention that I know mustangs better than any man you've got. And I know how to catch them. That's dollars in your pocket—good business."

"Now see here, boy!"

"You see here!" Jory swore. "Part of what you said was true. Only the part about *your* range isn't. Most of what you claim is government land and those mustangs got a right to be there. I'll go on catching them because I think good horses are needed in this country." Jory's eyes narrowed and his voice shook with cold anger. "But I won't catch mustangs so you can sell them for their hides, Mr. Hightower.

It's a bloody waste of good horseflesh. And I'm going to do everything I can to put you out of the business. Come on, Darby. Let's get out of here."

They were halfway across the room when Hightower raged and the tone of his voice stiffened Darby's back.

"Goddamn you misfits! You're walking dead. You and anyone who joins up against me are nothing but walking dead!"

Darby Buckingham paced back and forth in his hotel room. His mood was black and the Cuban cigar jutted out of the corner of his mouth forgotten and unlit. Yesterday, he'd been proud of the way Jory had stood up to Hightower, and the kid's words about driving the powerful rancher out of the mustanging business were fine and high-sounding.

But today was Sunday. Hench was gone and his threat was being repeated all over town. The chances of hiring another crew were absolutely nonexistent. And without riders, he and Jory weren't in the mustanging business. It didn't help his mood any when he realized he would be little if any help on a roundup.

Darby was so dispirited he even forgot lunch. He didn't mind being beaten so much as not even having a chance to try. Hightower must have guessed he'd be unable to recruit help. That was probably why the rancher had left them alone last night.

A knock sounded at his door and Darby stopped pacing. Jory Parnes pulled out his gun and slipped behind the bed. Darby tiptoed over to the corner of the room, picked up his shotgun and called, "Who is it?"

"Jerome Jerome."

"What do you want?"

"Huh?"

"I said," Darby yelled, "what do you want!"

"Have to speak up a little louder, Buckingham."

"Oh, for cripes sake, Darby. It's got to be him. Open up."

Darby tromped over to the door and flung it aside. It was,

indeed, Jerome Jerome. And, standing just down the hall-way with her hands on her hips in a manner that would have been provocative if she hadn't been glaring at him, was Magdalena Lamesa. Or Maggie, as Jory said she demanded to be called.

"Well, don't stand there staring at me. I'm only here 'cause Jerome Jerome asked me to tag along."

Jerome Jerome winked at Darby. "Wasn't the reason atall. She's sweet on Jory."

"Dangit, Horseface!" she squawked. "You say a fool thing like that again and I'll make you eat your chaw!"

Jerome Jerome laughed out loud. He *did* have a horse-face, Darby decided angrily as he yanked a handkerchief from his back pocket to wipe the tobacco off another ruined shirt. Maybe Jerome Jerome was crazy because he laughed even harder. Darby backpedaled into the room trying to get out of range.

They took it as an invitation and pursued the retreating writer.

"Maggie!" Jory shoved his gun back into his pants and smiled for the first time all day. Perhaps, Darby thought, Jerome Jerome was a little more shrewd than he appeared. If only he didn't chew tobacco!

Darby hit upon an idea. Quickly moving to his dresser, he located a cigar and offered it to the old mustanger. "All the way from Cuba. The best you can buy, I believe." Anything to keep his room from being sprayed.

Jerome Jerome reached out and his pale blue eyes wid-ened. "Well, thank you, sir. Don't mind if I do, sir. Don't mind atall."

Then, right before his horrified eyes, Darby saw the old goat shove the cigar between his yellow teeth, bite it in two and chew it up like candy.

"Gawd-damn, that's good!" And he crammed the last of it into his mouth and chomped contentedly. Darby had to sit down.

"Mr. Buckingham," Maggie said, "there's no sense in

beating around the sagebrush, so I'll speak for Jerome Jerome as well as myself."

"Deeply appreciated, young lady."

"What are you staring at?" she demanded.

"Your gun," Darby answered. "I'm not used to seeing a young lady with a pistol strapped to her side."

Maggie laughed outright. "Mister, I have a hunch you're not used to one hell of a lot of the things that go on in this part of the country." Her smile faded away and he saw her studying him intently. "You know," she said finally, "one of the reasons I want to work for you is just that I can't figure you at all. Jory says you whipped Paxton Bullock. And last night I heard about what you did to Hench and a couple of his bullies. But every time I look at you . . ."

"Yes?"

"I just can't believe what folks say. It's like there just *has* to be another fella with your name doing all those things. But good sense tells me there's nobody else in the world with a name like Darby Buckingham."

"Well," he said with more than a trace of irritation, "I'm afraid you'll have to work it all out for yourself, Miss Lamesa." He paused. "You say one of the reasons you want to work for me is curiosity. From the little Jory has told me, is it safe to say the other reason is to avenge your father?"

She wore a bandanna around her neck and Darby saw it move when she swallowed.

"That's right," she said quietly. "I've been waiting for a long time for a man to ride in and challenge Hench Hightower. And I promised myself that, no matter who or what he was, I'd join forces. I don't care about your money if that's a problem. Give whatever you think I've earned to Jerome Jerome here. He won't turn it down."

"That's a fact, I won't. Got any more of them cigars, Mr. Buckingham?"

"Uhh, I think I'm all out," Darby said quickly. The man's cheeks were so full he could barely talk, and worst of all, he was looking for a place to spit. Obviously, a decision had to be made. Darby glanced over toward Jory. "Well?"

"Hire them." Jory was watching the girl closely.

Darby sighed. Something told him he was making a big mistake. And even worse, he was going to spend a lot of evenings around the campfire feeding Cuban cigars to Jerome Jerome. But it was better than riding out of Elko without even putting up a fight. Blast! he thought. A kid whose only chance at survival was a sneak shot, a girl who was probably more lethal than Paxton Bullock and who was about to realize she had more weapons than she even dreamed, a damn cigar eater, and himself. The four of them were going to take on mustangs and a cattle baron intent on murder. But, he thought, trying to be philosophical, it ought to make one hell of a story.

His eyes skipped over each of them. "All right," he said. "First thing in the morning, we'll buy everything we need. I want to leave by midday."

"Yahoo!" Jerome Jerome bellowed as Darby covered his face. An idea! Maybe he should send this old devil out to talk to Paxton Bullock. Maybe Jerome Jerome had their most offensive weapon of all.

CHAPTER 8

Since early morning, he'd come to appreciate how much preparation it took to go mustanging. They'd assembled for breakfast and Darby's intentions were to make a general list of supplies and proceed to buy all that was necessary. But, as he sat over his coffee, it became apparent that a great deal had to be accomplished if they hoped to leave in the early afternoon. So he came up with an excellent plan. Each person was given the responsibility for a certain aspect of the trip. Jory's task was to buy pack horses and saddles. Jerome Jerome would gather all the materials necessary to erect a catch corral and holding pens—that meant hammers, nails, axes, and a couple of hundred feet of rope. Maggie's job was to buy enough food to last them at least two months, and Darby made it clear he wanted everyone to eat well.

For Darby's part, it was agreed he was doing plenty just paying for everything. The rest of the morning, while Jory, Maggie, and Jerome Jerome were scouring Elko for whatever they needed, Darby stayed in his hotel room and wrote.

First, he completed a long letter to Dolly Beavers, outlining their trip over from Running Springs and concluding about his troubles with Hench Hightower. He tried to make the letter sound both cheerful and optimistic and managed to imply he'd settled on a good crew, of sufficient size and ability, to handle any opposition from the powerful rancher. He felt a little guilty about misleading her that way, but determined that it was better than having her worry.

Actually, he discovered he missed Dolly considerably. True, she did have a most annoying way of dragging him to the floor whenever she saw the chance. And she gave him no privacy whatever. Yet, since leaving her, he'd often found himself remembering something they'd laughed about or just experienced. The woman had an undeniable charm and optimism upon which, if he wasn't careful, he could become dependent. There was no doubt that he would be glad to see her again—if he could.

He wrote a second letter to his publisher, J. Franklin Warner, outlining his story idea and promising that he would begin writing at once. And, true to his word, he did.

Darby finished the first chapter at noon and lit a cigar to celebrate. A young mustanger with a crippled right hand. Powerful adversaries to contend with. Magdalena Lamesa, a girl-woman who bore revenge in her heart and a Colt six gun on her shapely hip. Jerome Jerome, crazy, wild, and tough. Yes, he thought, puffing with satisfaction, it was all there and what made it especially rewarding was that it was true. Once again, he congratulated himself on the decision to leave New York and experience the West. Writing this story would be as easy as sipping good brandy; the problem was how it would all end.

That afternoon, they rode across the huge valley floor toward the rugged Independence Mountains. Darby had returned to his buckskins and was content to listen to the others talk. It amused him for a time to watch Jory and the girl make an elaborate show of mutual disinterest. Both were expending a great deal of effort to carry on a bantering conversation with Jerome Jerome, who seemed to be an encyclopedia of horse stories.

"You know the hardest kind of horse there is to catch?" Before anyone could answer, Jerome Jerome continued, "It's the *cimarrónes*, saddle horses that went wild. Once they get the taste of freedom, they're the craftiest animals I ever saw."

He spit a stream of tobacco at a rock and was dead center. "Ya see, they've been around cowboys and know how we think. You couldn't drive them into a corral with a tribe of Comanche Indians. You ever hear of the Murphy horses? Probably not," he grunted. "Well, the Murphy horses were a couple of geldings. And from what I been told, they were fine horses up until they got loose at the age of five or six. They joined a band up on Elko Mountain. That's mean country up there and those Murphy horses held it like a stronghold for nearly twenty years. They worked as a team and spelled each other as lookouts. Just the sight of a man going anywheres near the mountain and one of the Murphys would give a whistle and every animal in the herd was ready to bolt. A hell of a lot of good men went after them, but had no luck atall. When chased, the Murphys would split, each taking part of the herd along with them. They'd go down opposite sides of that mountain like goats and there wasn't a horse and rider alive could do it faster. When they hit the valley, they'd turn either east or west and start flying. After a couple of miles, they'd hightail it back up the mountain and have one hell of a big laugh together."

"What finally happened?" Darby asked.

A twinkle crept into Jerome Jerome's eye. "One day after a 'specially hard chase, those Murphys got together on top and thought it was so funny they plumb laughed themselves to death."

They made camp against the eastern base of the Independence Mountains and continued up their slopes at daybreak. It was country as inhospitable as any Darby had ever seen. Spewn with rocks and sharp ridges, covered with sage and juniper; he wondered how anything could survive. But they saw signs of mustangs everywhere. And when they finally crested the last summit, he saw another valley with miles of cottonwood trees tracing the path of a meandering stream.

"There," Jory said, pointing to the west, "the Tuscarora Mountains. One of the finest mustang ranges in Nevada. Paxton Bullock's territory."

"It's free country," Darby said, shading his eyes toward

the setting sun. "Are those Hightower cattle down below?"

"Yeah." Jory frowned. "He doesn't own that valley but his stock are scattered for at least fifteen miles through the meadows. At night, the mustangs filter off the ridges toward the creek. There are some good water holes up in the Tuscaroras, but they're mostly dry by late summer. And even if they weren't, that meadow grass below is the best feed in this part of the country."

"Where will we be working?" Maggie asked.

Jory shifted in his saddle. His expression grew thoughtful. "I'd say we should angle south. It's that much farther from Hightower headquarters and chock-full of wild horses. We'll find a canyon that leads down to water. I think I know of such a place. There's enough pine to cut corral poles and it's just out of the way enough so every mustang in this territory won't be watching us. We could work most of the summer and never see a Hightower rider."

"Then let's not go there," Maggie snapped. "Like Darby said, 'it's a free country.'"

They all turned toward Darby and he remembered that he was the boss. "It would seem to me," he said slowly, "that we're rather ill prepared to both wage a range war and catch mustangs. When we were riding out of Elko, I saw a look on everyone's face that said we weren't coming back." Darby's eyes covered them each in turn. "I'm not afraid of trouble, but if we could ride back into Elko with a string of mustangs, people might just start believing that we mean business. Perhaps then I can find additional riders who aren't afraid to join up with us. Does that make sense?"

Both Jerome Jerome and Jory nodded. But Darby could tell a struggle was going on within the girl.

"Aw, hell-fire," she finally said with great reluctance, "I guess I'm outvoted this time. But I think you men are wrong about one thing."

"What's that?" Darby asked.

Her expression was bleak and her voice was barely a whisper. "My father had the same idea. He was certain that if he shied clear of Hightower wranglers, they'd leave him be. They didn't. And it'll be the same way now. If any of you think he won't send out hunters in search of us, you're wrong. So keep your guns oiled, because he'll locate us within two weeks or my name ain't Maggie Lamesa."

"It isn't," Jory replied. "Your name is Magdalena and I like the sound of it."

If looks could turn a heart to stone, Darby thought, his young friend would be in another world. But Jory didn't let it faze him at all and Jerome Jerome probably hadn't even seen her because he started another story. Darby drummed the black gelding's rib cage and they descended toward the valley.

That night they camped under the cottonwood trees and Darby fell asleep listening to the sound of Hightower cattle bawling at the moon and stars. In the morning, he peeled off the buckskins and, with clenched teeth, followed Jory and the old mustanger into the creek. It might be weeks before they had another chance to bathe. Shivering in the cold morning sun, he decided it was just as well. Long before the sun was high, they were riding up into the Tuscaroras looking for Jory's hidden canyon. At noon, he saw his first band of mustangs.

They were on a mesa and he counted twelve. The mares were mostly bays and five had foals at their sides. But it was the stallion that caused Darby's pulse to quicken. Though the distance was at least a mile, he could see by the way the leader moved that every fiber in his muscular body was quivering. He was magnificent! Deep-chested, the stallion tossed his head at the wind and seemed to dance in the air as he moved back and forth between the intruders and his mares. His coat was rich copper and there was an air of majesty about the animal that electrified the space between them. Darby saw the horse shake its head, snake-like, in unspoken challenge.

"Yee-haw!" Jerome Jerome bellowed and before Darby quite knew what was happening, the crazy old man was spurring his horse up the hillside, waving his hat in circles and bellowing at the very top of his lungs.

The stallion reared, trumpeted a call, and then wheeled at his band. Like deer, they leapt from a standing position to full run and charged out of sight with their tails flying like banners.

At the top of the hill, Jerome Jerome hauled his mount to a sliding stop. "Yee-haw!" he roared, still waving his stetson wildly overhead. Then all was still and Darby saw Jerome Jerome come riding slowly back. The old man's face was creased with a grin from ear to ear and he was chewing tobacco and spitting at a ferocious rate.

Darby laughed outright. Now the last piece of the puzzle was in place. Jory's and Maggie's reasons he'd understood, but Jerome Jerome, he hadn't been sure about. He was now. The old man was as happy as a child at Christmas. His motive was as pure as the scent of pine over the Tuscaroras—he had a lifelong case of mustang fever.

They found Jory's canyon and even Jerome Jerome grunted with approval. Darby judged it to be perhaps six or seven miles long, sloping down toward the valley. A series of three ridges cut across the canyon's head and all were heavily timbered. The ridges were important according to Jory. He explained to Darby that mustangs instinctively sought higher ground when chased. They'd stick to the ridges until they found themselves running out of ground on the canyon floor. Once they were heading down toward the valley, they'd be on open ground and could be kept from breaking into the wooded canyonsides. What really made Jory's choice excellent was that the canyon, at its narrowest point, formed a dogleg before widening again at the valley opening. That was where they'd build their corral—where the canyon walls were less than fifty feet apart.

The unsuspecting mustangs would be caught before they had a chance to realize their mistake and scatter or turn back on the riders. But it was going to take a lot of work to set up a catch corral wide enough to reach the narrow canyon walls. They would start building at once.

During the following days, Darby worked as hard as he'd ever in his life. His job was to climb up into the hillsides and cut trees that couldn't be seen from below. Maggie would shake out her lariat and drag them through the timber parallel to the valley floor where the two mustang men would pack them up on horses and haul them down to the canyon's mouth. Both Jory and Jerome Jerome were adamant that no signs of anything being cut or dug should be visible, and each evening they took turns riding up to the ridges and inspecting the hillsides. If the mustangs even sensed a corral, their entire effort would be wasted.

That first night, after cutting trees all day, Darby was in a state of exhaustion. And, the next morning, he had to grit his teeth to endure the pains in his lower back. His arms and shoulders were fine. Lifting kept them hard as rock and capable of doing monumental tasks. But his back did ache and his hands were blistered raw.

Jerome Jerome told him that horse urine was the best medicine for toughening up his hands and building calluses. Darby told the old man what he could do with that idea in no uncertain terms. Well, then, the second best thing was chewing tobacco. The next day, Darby chewed and spit up two Cuban cigars. It offended him deeply.

Each evening, just before sunset, Darby would ride back to camp wondering if it was all worth-while. He'd never dreamed catching mustangs could be so much trouble. And the very thought that a single mistake could ruin it all was enough to make him shudder. But when he walked through the canyon's mouth and saw the two horsemen working without letup, his resolve stiffened and he felt ashamed that only his back ached and blisters formed on blisters. Besides, the corral was something to raise pride in all of them.

Extending from each side of the canyon walls, the enclosure was bag-shaped and the rails were at least seven feet high. Jerome Jerome knew that with anything shorter the stallion could fly over it like an eagle followed by his mares.

They set the posts three feet deep and in ground so hard that Jory's pick sometimes bounced out of the hole. Darby, watching the young man swinging against the rocky soil, placed his ax down and took charge of the hole digging. His technique wasn't much, but with his weight and strength, he managed to average a steady three postholes an hour. By the end of the first week, his back had stopped aching, the palms of his hands were healing, and he had Jerome Jerome stitch a band of leather through his pants to keep them from falling off.

On the last day, when enough timber had been cut and Maggie had hauled it down to the corral, they finished in the early afternoon and climbed the canyonside to inspect their work. It was a hard climb, but Darby found he barely exerted himself. He hadn't been so strong and fit since his fighting days.

"Well," he said, addressing them, "I don't know the difference between a good and a bad corral, but it seems to me we've done a fine job."

Jory smiled. "It's good all right. Paxton always was mighty particular about his corrals but we never built one to match that."

Maggie brushed a tendril of hair back from her eyes and looked across the canyon toward the Tuscaroras. "I'm surprised he hasn't come by to tear it down. We've been here long enough for him to get back from Cheyenne. And hunting us will be his first order of business."

They were feeling good and proud of the work they'd done and Darby didn't want the thought of Hightower or Paxton Bullock to ruin the mood. They were all tired; he could see it in Jory's and Maggie's young faces. Even Jerome Jerome seemed to have aged visibly these past few days, although Darby had given him the easier job of nailing the cross poles. But it still involved continuous lifting, and fourteen-hour workdays left their mark.

"Tell you what," Darby said, throwing an arm across the

old man's shoulders, "I've got a good bottle of brandy down in camp and a cigar or two that you could eat. Let's celebrate."

"Fittin'," Jerome Jerome said quietly and without as much enthusiasm as Darby had hoped. He turned to Jory and the girl. "Since you young ones neither smoke, chew cigars, nor drink, I'm not sure what you can do to join in the festivities."

Jory glanced over at Maggie. She looked away quickly. That wasn't like her. Maggie Lamesa normally had a smart answer for everything. Jory smiled. "You and Jerome Jerome go on down, we'll be along to see you don't get carried away with the celebrating."

"Maggie?" Darby stepped up to her. "You seem unusually quiet. Is something wrong?"

"No," she said pensively, "I was just looking at our corral and thinking how it was . . . well, kind of fun working together." She looked him straight in the eye. "I'm going to have to stop thinking so much."

"Why?"

"I can't seem to shake the feeling that Hightower men are in these hills. And that they've just been waiting until we're finished."

Darby scowled. Though no one had seen a trace of another human since the day they'd arrived, everyone kept a rifle very close at hand. "You're tired, Maggie. We all are and tomorrow we do nothing but rest. Sleep under a tree. How does that sound?"

"It sounds like a danged good idea." Surprisingly, she reached up and gently pulled at his beard. It was meant to be a playful gesture, but it didn't quite succeed in dispelling the melancholy.

Darby wondered if perhaps she was thinking about her father. How he must have built corrals like the one below. How, as a child, she may have helped him.

"Jory," she said, "why don't you go with them and make sure they don't get into trouble."

He hid his disappointment well. "Sure. What about you?"

"I'm going to hike up to a spring I noticed just above. I need a good cold bath to shake me out of the mood I'm in. Don't worry, I'll be along."

Darby looked up at the spring. It wasn't far. Only a couple of hundred yards. He couldn't see water, but the thickets and patch of grass left no doubt she was right. In a way, he felt a little like her father, just as he sometimes found himself thinking of Jory as his son. "All right. But don't stay long. The sun will be going down in another hour and we wouldn't want to have to come searching for you in the dark."

"Speak for yourself," Jory said with a laugh.

"Maybe you two better watch *him*," she said with a wink that caused everyone to smile. "I've got a woman's guess he isn't as tired as he looks!"

Almost a half mile away, at the very crest of the steep canyon wall, hidden in a thick stand of juniper, Paxton Bullock lay belly-down on a flat rock. His big shoulders were bunched forward and he adjusted the field glasses with care.

"What are they doin'!" a voice graveled from behind.

"They're talking. That's all. Wait a minute. One of them is coming up the hill. Why, that goddamn Buckingham hired a boy!"

"Boy or not, you know that won't change the way Hench wants us to handle this. Our orders are to kill them all."

"Shut up!" Paxton swore. "I can't talk and look at the same time. Go on back and tell the rest I'll be along in a while."

He leaned forward, watching the boy climb toward the spring. He saw the figure bend at the edge of the water and drink. Paxton felt his anger building. He'd kill them as ordered, but it stuck in his craw to do it to a boy who, by his size, probably wasn't more than fourteen or fifteen. A damn shame. Yet, there could be no loose ends. No witnesses.

The kid stood up and swept off his hat. Then Paxton took a sharp intake of breath as he saw the figure unwind strands of hair until it cascaded below the shoulders. Before he could quite understand, the figure began to disrobe and Paxton leaned forward until his elbows pinched on the rock from his weight. It wasn't a boy and it certainly wasn't a little girl. What he saw sent his pulse racing. It was Maggie Lamesa and he was probably the only man alive who knew that she was now a woman.

Time passed and the sun slid behind the hills as he watched her walk slowly down toward the canyon bathed in a crimson sunset. His throat ached worse than his elbows. Paxton Bullock realized he'd never seen anything so damned pretty.

She was lithe, straight, and clean. She shone against the sunset. At twenty-eight, he'd visited his share of ladies on back-alley streets but he'd never seen anything like this.

Maybe it was the sunset that made it seem as though this was a sign for him and him alone. Whatever, Paxton Bullock felt something inside stir that had never stirred before. And to him, Maggie Lamesa seemed to hold all the promise of goodness in his life. Without consciously thinking about it, he reached for her in his mind like a small child might do the first time he sees a star. He thought nothing of what it could mean for the girl. Only himself. And it never would have occurred to the rough gunman that he was the man who had killed her father. No, all that seemed to matter as he lay on that Tuscarora hillside was that she would be his; he barely was able to stay down on the rock and keep from charging after her.

For Paxton, it wasn't love or infatuation. It was just a gut twisting, sweaty-palm wanting. And that . . . that was all that was necessary.

When she reached camp and the sun was so low he couldn't track her with the glasses any longer, Paxton slumped down on the rock with a sigh. Somehow. Someway.

He *had* to have that girl for himself. And if that meant going up against Hench, then God help the old man because he was going to do it. He'd seen Maggie as no other man had—and it was going to stay that way—or else.

CHAPTER 9

Darby Buckingham didn't have to ask if this was the band of mustangs they wanted; he could tell it by the expression on Jerome Jerome's face.

The wild horses were across the ridge and slightly to the north. They were about four miles from the head of the canyon; then it would be another three miles to the catch corral.

Jerome Jerome slid back into the trees and they followed. Though they'd gone over their plan several times, Darby was the only one without experience and he wanted to make sure he understood exactly what each one of them was going to do.

"My role," he said, "is to go straight back to the canyon. I'm to hide my horse just below the corral and then take cover beside the gate. The moment the stallion enters, I start to move."

"That's right," Jory said. "Remember that I'll be riding on their tails. By the time that stallion realizes he's trapped, it will be too late for him to turn back until he's inside the corral. But he will turn back. And fast. That's why you've *got* to close the gate before he can come back through his herd. Because, if he sees a way out, even a few feet of open daylight, he'll charge that gate so hard we'd be picking you up on the next ridge."

"I see," Darby replied. "My part, however, does seem comparatively simple."

"Don't you believe it," Maggie said quickly. "The man at the gate has to move fast and have enough nerve to slam the opening shut in the face of the stallion's charge." Her voice was low and very serious. "We'll be doing the hard riding because the three of us are better on a horse."

"No argument there," Darby said agreeably.

"But," she continued, "your job is far more dangerous. The only thing that can go wrong for us is that our horses might fall. Still, we'd have a chance, because we'll be chasing those mustangs. That's not true for the man at the gate. If you're slow, they'll charge the opening like Jory said and you'll likely be knocked down and trampled. The same can happen if you falter, stumble, or can't get the damned thing closed. Any of those things, Darby, and there won't be enough left of you to bury."

Darby understood perfectly. He knew exactly where he'd lie in wait. It was a hole very near the gate, right at the foot of the canyonside. They'd dug it out of rock and had had to settle for a depth of less than four feet. But there was enough room inside to crouch down out of sight and he'd practiced getting out as fast as he could. Jory told him to wait until the very last second, when it seemed that the mustangs were right on top of him, before he jerked up. Then, as they swept by, to jump and run. The gate was long and heavy, he was really the only one of the four with enough strength to hit it running and bull it shut. Over and over, he'd rehearsed his moves until he could do it with his eyes closed. And he just might have to. There were twenty-six horses in the herd and the dust would be thick.

"We'd better start," Jory said. He looked over and spoke to Maggie and Jerome Jerome. "Give us about an hour to get in position. It'll take you that long to ride downwind far enough. Once you get them running, they'll stay to the ridge until it peters out at the head of our canyon. That's a long stretch and your horses will be getting winded. They'll start down the canyon, then I'll take over. I'll come busting in, yelling and shooting, and push them right on down toward the corral. They won't try to turn on me because they'll see their escape as being the valley."

Jerome Jerome spat tobacco juice. "We won't be that far

behind you, sonny. If they turn, Maggie and I will be ready. Now, if we're finally done palaverin', let's ride."

"Look!" Paxton said quickly.

"Where's the boy and the old man?"

Paxton grinned, his lean face wolfishly eager. "They're getting ready to drive mustangs, stupid. Ahh! There. I knew Jory would be the last rider. He always did figure that position is the touchiest."

"What about the other man?"

"The Easterner?" Paxton's lips curled with scorn and open hatred. Ever since their fight, he'd been dreaming of the day when he could get even. And this was it. They'd be almost directly below when the mustangs came storming toward the mouth of the canyon. Almost nothing in the world would have given him more pleasure than to kill them both. Yet, there was one problem that stopped him—Magdalena Lamesa. He hadn't been able to get her off his mind for a single minute in the three days since he'd watched her on the hillside.

Standing on the canyon's rim, he knew exactly what would happen below. The woman and the old man would drive the mustangs toward Jory and he'd take them right past Hightower rifle sights. Shooting the Easterner and Jory would be as easy as falling off a horse. But that didn't make his task of saving Magdalena any easier. Someway, he had to make damn sure she never reached this point.

So far, he hadn't told any of the rest that the smallish figure was a woman. He was afraid they'd shoot her anyway because they'd all heard Hench's orders to kill everyone— leave no witnesses. They hadn't seen her like he had and they wouldn't understand. They'd take it as a sign of weakness, and Paxton knew it was very dangerous to have men such as he ramrodded thinking their boss was vulnerable. There were four crews on the Hightower payroll and each one was headed by the meanest, toughest, fastest man with a gun who could be found.

Hench himself made it damn good and clear that the ramrodding jobs were always open to anyone strong enough to take them. That's why Paxton never really eased up, nor hesitated to make a show of force. Up to now, it had worked. Still, there were a couple of men on his crew, Tyson and Hart, whom he thought were possibly as fast as he was. But they were cautious and he wanted to make sure they stayed that way. If he showed a weakness, they might decide to give him a try. Paxton was no coward, far from it, but he was no fool either. He was pushing thirty and he wasn't going to get any better with his fists or six-shooter. He just wanted them to think he liked to use both, and perhaps he did. Jory Parnes had been his latest demonstration.

So it was that he made his plan carefully. "Tyson, Hart, you and everyone else grab your rifles and spread out along the top of this rim. Don't shoot until Jory passes below. Then, when the mustangs go into the corral, open fire on both of them."

Bill Tyson, a short, blocky young man with reddish hair and deep-set eyes, glanced at Bud Hart, then looked back. "That's plain enough," he said tonelessly. "What about the kid and the old man?"

"I'll take care of them," Paxton replied. The very fact that Tyson would ask galled him to quick anger. But, for once, he bit it down. They were running out of time and the last thing he needed was trouble from his own. Still, he made a note that Tyson needed to be taught a lesson, and soon.

Paxton drew his gun and saw with some amusement that both Tyson and Hart stiffened. He pretended to check the cylinder load, then shoved the gun back into his holster. He'd made his point. "I'll ride up through the trees," he said casually, "then cut them off from behind. I want to make damn sure no one escapes."

"You won't have need for that gun—today," Tyson said, emphasizing the last word, "ain't none of 'em going to be riding out alive."

Paxton started for his horse. He believed Tyson; there was

no way that Jory or Buckingham could get out of the canyon. He climbed into his saddle, dismissing the two as already dead. What concerned him now was the woman. Magdalena couldn't be allowed to get past him or she'd be riddled like the others. He had to save her, but that meant dealing with Jerome Jerome first.

As he guided his horse toward the top of the canyon, Paxton mulled over the steps he would take. Jerome Jerome was no stranger to these parts and Paxton knew the old mustanger was both a little crazy and very dangerous with a rifle. A sense of urgency gripped Paxton as he thought he heard shots to the south. Time was running out. He dismounted and tied his horse in a concealing stand of trees. Yanking his Winchester out of its scabbard, he hurried along the ridge, stopping every few paces to check the line of fire. It had to be perfect.

He came to a pair of shoulder-high rocks and stepped in behind them. Very carefully, he held the rifle up, sighting on the canyon below. His field of vision between the rocks was at least eighty yards; that was plenty of distance to take aim and fire twice. The old man and Magdalena wouldn't know what hit them.

Less than a mile away and also in hiding, Maggie Lamesa felt the horse tremble with excitement. "Easy, easy," she whispered softly. "We've done this before."

But she tried not to think of those days when she had been a small girl on a big horse and so scared she'd had to grip the saddle horn to keep from shaking. Fenton Lamesa trusted her then, even if she was just a little girl. First, just like now, she'd heard them coming, a low, hard drubbing sound that grew and grew until—suddenly—the mustangs seemed to burst from the land. Manes and tails flying, legs moving so swiftly they blurred over the earth and carried all that thunder and sound sweeping along before them. It was a sight a person would remember forever and feel blessed to have had the experience.

But now she waited, seeming not even to breathe, so great was the excitement within her. Wait. Wait until they were close—then, a slice of the quirt and the animal beneath her vaulting out of cover. The mustangs kept running at her. Shout. Wave your hat. Fire your gun. Anything, but please, God, make them turn. And they did! Every time.

And then, they were sliding off to the side and she could see Fenton with a look as wild as that of the mustangs. Together, they would run. Her father and the mustangs and they'd chase them down to the trap and . . .

There! Right out of the ground. Charging. Only she wasn't a little girl now. Wait. Wait! Go!

Maggie chopped her horse across the rump and they leapt out with the mustangs tearing forward as though they didn't see her or didn't care.

She yanked her hat from her head and gave a wild yell that was drowned in the thunder of hoofbeats. They turned. They always turned and she saw the stallion cut away with his nostrils flared and his ears laid down tight.

Her mount fought for its head, wanting to run past them, but she curbed it in, letting them charge by. And there . . . there was Jerome Jerome. For one moment, as the rider emerged from the dust, standing tall in his stirrups and shouting at the top of his lungs, Maggie saw Fenton once more. What a picture! Hair streaming back, mouth open in some kind of triumphant shout, magnificently alive . . .

"Yee-haw! Yee-haw!" he bellowed again and again. "Yee . . ."

Maggie saw him lift even higher in his stirrups. So high he seemed to hang spread-eagled in the mountain air. "Haw!"

Then, his head snapped back and he began his dead fall.

Though her own horse was veering away, she saw the loose, terrible way he struck the canyon floor; and he rolled over and over before he came to rest faceup to the sky. His horse, reins trailing and stirrups banging it on, stampeded by her and into the herd.

For a moment, fear paralyzed her. Then she was hauling

her mount to a stop. Turning back, but not wanting to. Her
mind was blank. She'd heard no shot, but how could she
have?

Then what! "Jerome," she cried, wheeling her horse back.
"Oh, Jerome!"

Suddenly Maggie heard the rifles. It sounded like an
army. For one awful second she wasn't sure what to do.

But Paxton did. He'd seen the way his rifle slug had hit
the old mustanger square in the chest. There was no mistak-
ing the shot. A man didn't get thrown out of his saddle like
that unless he was dead before he struck earth.

He swung his Winchester and watched Magdalena reining her horse around just as he'd known she would. When
the shots off the canyonsides began, he saw her head turn.
That's when he drilled in his second rifle bullet.

It caught her horse in midstride. He saw the animal stagger. Almost fall. He fired again and the horse's front legs
collapsed and it went down, spilling its rider hard.

The horse was dead and probably had been with the first
bullet. Paxton scrambled around the rocks and raced for his
own mount, fighting through brush. A fall like Magdalena
had taken could kill or cripple. But there'd been no choice.
Both she and the old man would have opened fire. Struggling for breath, he reached his horse and swung into the
saddle. The odds were that she was alive, perhaps only
stunned by the fall. He hoped so; it seemed as though everything he wanted depended on that small bit of luck.

He whipped his mount down the canyonside with rocks
and gravel coming down with him. Twice, his horse almost
fell, but somehow he reached flat ground and spurred mer-
cilessly on. Then, just as suddenly, he tore at the reins and
forced the horse to a sliding stop and was on the ground
running. But what he saw turned his long legs to mush and
he froze, still fifty feet from Magdalena Lamesa.

She was hurt. It made him sick but he couldn't move.
There she was, crawling outstretched, pushing forward inch

by inch. He didn't hear the gunfire down canyon anymore. Somehow, he willed himself to walk toward her even as she continued to crawl away. She was sobbing, her head was up and turned toward the old mustanger's body.

For the first time in his life, Paxton felt a surge of remorse that almost brought him to his knees. He followed her slowly, like a dog. His stomach was sick and a lump the size of his own fist seemed to fill his throat. She wasn't beautiful now. One side of her face was scraped and bleeding, and her left arm was twisted so that she couldn't use it to pull herself forward. And the sound she made forced him to clench his teeth and want to cry out toward the sky. He'd never heard anything like it.

Not a sob, nor a wailing sound, but something that had to come from her depths like that of a wounded animal. Over and over, she kept saying it and he tried to understand. Jerome, Jerome? Jory, Jory? Too strangled to tell. All he knew for certain was that it was a terrible sound, more primitive in its pain than he'd ever thought a human could make.

Foot by foot, she drew herself across the hoof-scarred earth. And he followed, wondering what he could say or do to stop that sound, to make her, once again, the shining, beautiful woman on the mountainside.

Slowly, he walked around in front of her and stood rooted. He saw her movement stop and the sound in her throat rattled to silence. She stared at his boots for what seemed like a long time, then her gaze inched up his legs until her face was upraised toward his. He tried to speak then, to say something, anything, to chase away the wildness he saw. But his throat seemed as though it were knotted, and he gagged.

He knelt down in front of her, pulling a handkerchief from around his neck. She was his now. Why did his hand shake so hard when he reached out to wipe the blood from the side of her face?

"Magdalena," he rasped, "I've come to take care of you."

She blinked, her eyes widened with a flicker of recognition. Then, he recoiled as he saw her lips pull back from her teeth in something that he could only interpret as a snarl.

She tried to rip his hand from her face and he heard bones in her shoulder grate. Before he could move, he saw pain glaze her eyes and she slumped forward, unconscious.

Paxton sagged on his knees. What else could he have expected? Did she know that he'd been the one who'd killed her father? She couldn't. Yet, those eyes and the way they burned with hatred!

He turned away from her to stare at the hillside. He remembered how she looked, unclothed and glistening in the sunset. And he knew, deep inside, he would never be able to blot out that image as long as he drew a breath. It *was* a sign, by God! Never mind what he'd just seen in her eyes. She would change. He would keep her until she did. Like a mustang that Jory Parnes took a special liking to, he'd stay with her, gentle her with words and a soft touch. She'd change. She *had* to become his woman. Maybe it wasn't hate he'd seen, but pain. Yes, that was it! Her shoulder. He'd nurse her back to health and she'd forgive him. Then he'd take her for his own.

The running thunder of mustangs jarred him out of his thoughts. Paxton glanced back down the forgotten canyon and saw them returning! They were close—too close. His ground-tied horse bolted away in fear. Paxton swept the woman up in his arms and froze for one awful second while he weighed his choices. If he tried to reach the side of the canyon, he'd never make it carrying Magdalena. His only chance was to jump behind her dead horse and hope that the mustangs would veer away from the blood smell.

He sprinted to the fallen animal and shoved Maggie in close to the animal's underside. Then, he pulled his weapon and fired at the sky, shouting at the top of his lungs.

The mustangs were sluggish with exhaustion. They passed by and he heard the wind tearing in and out of their lungs.

He slumped down beside her in relief. At last, everything was quiet. Out of the corner of his eye, something made him

jump. It was the face of Maggie's horse. In death, the animal's lips were pulled back in what looked like a snarl, just
as hers had been.

For some reason, it rattled him more than it should.
He staggered to his feet, picked up the girl, and hurried toward the canyonside. He had an overpowering urge to leave
this place.

Up above, his men would be waiting for orders. And those
orders would be to ride away from all this back to Hightower's ranch. And there, he knew, lay the final obstacle he
had to overcome if he was to have this woman.

At the top of the canyon, his men were standing in silence. None of them had said anything about Magdalena.
And they avoided his eyes when he challenged them to
speak.

Paxton took one man's horse without asking. He lifted the
woman into the saddle and mounted behind. Just before
he reined away from the canyon below, he took a final
glance.

Jory was easy to locate. He'd been shot from his horse,
then trampled. The Easterner lay beside the corral gate.
Nothing moved. All was deathly still.

"Let's ride," Paxton said to the others.

Bill Tyson spurred his horse by. "Hench ain't going to let
her live," he called back.

Paxton stiffened. This was no time for trouble. Not with
Magdalena. And Tyson was right; everyone on the Hightower payroll knew the penalty of going against an order. A
chill passed through his body and he hugged the young
woman a little tighter. When they reached headquarters, he
knew whose side the men he rode with would be on. They'd
go with the one who paid their wages—and he'd go it alone
against them all.

CHAPTER 10

Darby was hiding, like a marmot in its burrow, when he first heard the mustangs coming down the valley. Keeping low and not risking a peek at the sight was the hardest thing he'd done in a long time. He could picture the scene as the band of horses raced toward where he crouched in wait. Nostrils distended with the need for air, manes and tails flying. The stallion was probably in the lead and he would look magnificent. Darby could almost feel the ground begin to shake, and he cursed his lot for not being able to see the wild horses as they swept closer and closer.

Then he heard the shots. Faintly, barely distinguishable over the thundering roll of hoofbeats. For a moment, he almost panicked, his mind jumping at once to Paxton Bullock. But, just in time, he froze. Of course! The gunfire would be coming from Jory and Jerome Jerome as they drove the mustangs down canyon.

So he stayed down, feeling the pounding of his own heart racing time with the mustangs. Wait, Jory had said, over and over. Wait until you know they are on you. When you can taste their dust, smell the horse sweat, feel the ground almost start to roll, hear them breathe, then move!

He did. Up from the hole he reared, engulfed in dust as they swept by. He ran for the corral gate side by side with the last of the mustangs. It was as though they didn't see him, only their escape between the narrow canyon walls.

He was at the gate, rooting it from the ground, bulling it closed.

"Darby! Take cover!"

The voice rose above the din and he twisted back. Not sixty feet away was Jory, his expression wild but not with exhilaration. Darby barely understood his words, but the split-second image of Jory's face told him everything. Jory's gun was in his hand and his horse was fighting wildly. He fired up at the canyon rim and Darby saw gun smoke blossom whitely against the trees.

Then, Jory's horse started to fall and Darby had an image of the young man kicking out from his stirrups and going down.

That's when the stallion struck him with the forgotten gate still half open. There was only a split-second awareness of what happened next. Darby was going to leave the gate, somehow reach Jory Parnes. But everything went too fast.

When the stallion and his mares barreled through the gate, they hit it so hard it tore from its leather hinges and knocked Darby flat. Just before the horses streamed back out, he saw Jory take another shot at the canyonside. And Darby marveled that he didn't turn his gun on the stallion, which was almost on top of him. That was his last thought as a terrible weight crushed him into the valley floor.

Five minutes later, when the dust had settled and the sound of hoofbeats had receded back up the canyon to the ridges beyond, the two friends lay still and covered with dirt.

He felt as though he were buried in the little hole beside the catch gate. The pain came in waves so strong he seemed to lift from his hole, then crash back down inside.

But, gradually, the pain subsided and he knew where he was, and slowly Darby Buckingham put the pieces back together. And as each one fit, memory returned to force him back to reality. He tried to push himself over, but couldn't. Dispassionately, he considered the possibility that he was paralyzed. Yet, he had to try. Slowly, like a man awaking from a deep, troubled dream, he rolled sideways, then pushed the heavy gate aside.

"Jory?" he whispered into the night. "Jory!"

Darby ached everywhere, and when he tried to stand, his

legs failed. Numb from their entrapment, he rubbed them until the circulation buzzed and he tried to stand again. This time he was successful, and he staggered forward toward the place where he'd seen the young man fall.

There was no fury, no revenge in him. That would come later. All he felt was pain and dread that he would find them all dead. Jory, the girl, Jerome Jerome. They'd hired on to help him and Darby felt desolate that he'd let them be slaughtered.

He groped forward. The moon was just a thin yellow wedge against a cold, starry sky, and in the canyon, it was as dark as a pit. His boot nudged something soft. "Jory?"

Darby fell to his knees. His hand brushed over the body, found the wrist. A pulse! He wanted to shout with happiness! But he felt something else too, and he knew it was blood. With a trembling hand, Darby examined the head and face and was relieved to discover no wounds. But he needed light! Badly.

He slipped one arm under Jory's knees, the other beneath his arms and lifted him from the ground as easily as most men would a small child. Then, he started toward their camp less than a mile away. There he would take care of Jory, save his life if it could yet be saved.

He finished cleaning and bandaging Jory's wounds just as the sun rose to flood the valley. Darby tossed the last of their supply of wood on the fire, which had given him enough light to work by and heat to erase the cold night air.

Jory had three nasty-looking bullet wounds on his slender body, but none was fatal or even critical. One sliced across his hip, another the fleshy part of his right forearm. The third bullet was the most serious. It had burrowed up along the rib cage, lodging almost at the underarm. Jory had lost a great deal of blood and Darby worked feverishly to stop the bleeding. He had the sick feeling that the slug had probably cracked several ribs along its path.

Now, as the light grew stronger, he had one more task to

finish and that was to extract the bullet. He'd located a thick hunting knife and seared it against the fire until it was black. Then he wiped it across his sleeve and poured brandy over the blade, listening to it sizzle. Though the night air was still chill, sweat popped from every pore in his body. He pulled the bandage away and swallowed hard. At least the bullet was close to the surface, he could easily see the lump it made under Jory's arm.

Darby looked upward at the sunrise, said a prayer, and drew the knife blade across three inches of skin, pressing it right down to the rib.

Jory thrashed and moaned, but Darby held him pinned on the blanket. "Just one second more," he gritted. Then, with the point of the knife, he made two deft movements and popped the slug out. "There!"

But Jory didn't hear him. He'd lapsed back into unconsciousness. Darby moved even more quickly. He doused the incision with brandy and pressed the bandage down firmly. For half an hour, he held it that way. His eyes were vacant, unseeing and fixed up the canyon where he must soon go looking for Maggie and Jerome Jerome. He was sure he would find them dead.

He was just as sure that he could count on his fingers the number of days that remained in the life of Hench Hightower. He'd probably never find out whose bullets did what damage. All he could know for certain was that Hench gave the order. To Darby, that was as good as his death sentence.

He eased the pressure on Jory's wound and the bandage stuck with coagulated blood. Darby gently wrapped strips of blanket around the young man's ribs and tied them snugly in place. Then he stood up and took a long pull on the bottle of brandy. Its warmth ran through him like a river of flowing lava.

"Rest, my young friend," he whispered. "This won't take long."

By midmorning, he was starting back toward camp. He'd buried Jerome Jerome in the hole by the gate. Buried him sitting up and facing the narrow rock passage. In time, the corral would weather and fall. Mustangs would become accustomed to it and pass by on their way to the valley below. Darby figured the old mustanger would approve of his resting place and be happiest near the wild horses he'd loved to chase.

The disappearance of Magdalena Lamesa was a mystery. He'd stripped her horse of its saddle and found no evidence of blood. The mustangs had wiped out any hope of finding some clue as to what might have happened to the girl. Darby scouted the surrounding canyonsides in the hope she might be hiding or hurt and unable to answer his calls. But she'd vanished.

As he plodded wearily back toward camp with Maggie's saddle, bridle, and horse blankets, Darby tried to guess what might have become of her. Of one thing he was certain, she wouldn't have run out on them. The only possible explanation was that she'd been taken by Hightower's men. But why? If she was alive, she was a witness to the ambush and it made no sense at all, from Hightower's standpoint, to spare her. One thing for sure, if they believed she would remain quiet, even under threat of death, they were totally mistaken. He hadn't known her long, but long enough to realize the strength of Maggie Lamesa's will and her commitment to see Hightower brought to justice.

If Maggie was alive, it would be the nail that would seal Hightower's coffin. From where he and Jory had been fired upon, neither of them had seen faces. Only Maggie could give eyewitness proof that would finally topple the rancher's empire. Darby quickened his pace. He had to find that girl!

Back in camp, Jory was awake, but very weak. Darby realized that, no matter how desperate he was to find Maggie, they wouldn't be able to leave for several days. And first, they needed horses or at least one horse to carry Jory. He'd never be able to make it back to town on foot.

Jory stared at him with pain-glazed eyes as Darby told how he'd buried the old mustanger. "And I'm going up there and knock a gap in that fence so the mustangs can pass down to drink," Darby ended.

The young man nodded with patience. His mouth worked nervously and Darby realized Jory was waiting to hear about Maggie but was deathly afraid to ask.

"She's all right," he said.

"She is!"

Jory's face came alive and Darby smiled, then told him what he'd found and decided. During all this time, Jory never interrupted but listened intently until he was finished.

"Why?"

"I'm not sure," Darby said truthfully. "It doesn't make sense. Not now, at least. But I'll find out."

"No! We'll both find out."

Darby nodded. The young horseman was flat on his back and half-dead but his spirit burned inside.

"We're in love," Jory whispered.

"So I guessed. Don't worry, if they had meant to kill her, she would have been up in the canyon with Jerome Jerome. She's alive and, together, we will find her."

"At Hightower headquarters," Jory gritted.

"Of course," Darby replied, "of course. We'll return to Elko and have the doctor take a look at you first. Then I'll have the sheriff ride out with us."

"He won't want any part of it," Jory said, biting sarcasm in his voice.

Darby's fists clenched. "He'll come. One way or the other. He'll come and arrest Hightower or my name isn't Darby Buckingham!"

Jory leaned back to rest. "You know what I'm afraid of?"

"No, what?"

"I'm scared she's going to get herself killed because she hates him so much. She won't be able to keep quiet."

Darby sighed. "She's not stupid, Jory. If she thinks for even a moment, she'll realize she's the witness who can put Hightower on the gallows along with Paxton Bullock. I just hope she thinks about that. Everything depends on her now. She's *got* to think!"

Paxton saw his boss standing before the big stone house with his thumbs hooked in his gun belt. Beside him were a pair of men whom he recognized at once. Rio and Chesterton were worthless in every respect but one—gunfighting. Paxton had loathed them from the moment they'd hired on, and since that time, nothing had changed his initial reaction.

Rio was the taller, but Chesterton was the leader. Together, they did little but swagger and burn gunpowder in a constant effort to hone their skills. Paxton saw them as a couple of useless dogs that licked and scraped after a master and treated everyone else like scum. They ate with Hightower and slept in the main house like pampered hounds. Before their arrival, Paxton had often enjoyed his meals at the house. But no longer. Rio and Chesterton had a way of making other men lose their appetites. And they didn't know anything about cattle or horses. Nothing at all. They wore leather gloves when they rode and both looked bad in the saddle. But not on foot. As much as Paxton hated to admit it, wherever they walked, people stepped aside. He had a hunch that even Hightower didn't care much for them. They didn't *act* like men—more like tools, just bloodless, vacant-eyed tools made for killing. Many a time, Paxton had watched them practice throwing small things into the sky and shooting them to pieces. To his eye, Chesterton was a shade faster and that was probably why he was the unspoken leader. But the difference was so small the eye couldn't be sure. Paxton would have given money to see them go against one another. He was sure they'd both get off bullets like a single clap of thunder and there would be no victor. Rio and Chesterton were in a class all by themselves. That alone was reason enough for his hatred.

Paxton felt his stomach tighten as he rode nearer. Maybe Hench would understand about Magdalena. Surely he wouldn't have her killed. Not a woman! But as the distance closed, he saw Hench shift with irritation, slap his thigh in a gesture that Paxton knew meant he was mad. Damn mad. Rio and Chesterton acted upon the signal and dropped their boredom routines. They scented trouble.

Sweat rivered down his back. Paxton knew he was outmatched against either. While he was very fast, he was still a workingman. His hands were tough and calloused because Hightower paid him to catch mustangs, not practice with a six gun all day. He squeezed Magdalena a little tighter and knew he had to have a big edge or they'd both be dead very soon. He noted that Hench was armed too, but that didn't mean much. He was an old man who had once been good but gunfighting was a young man's game and Hench's reflexes were as brittle as his bones.

Paxton swore inwardly as they grew inexorably closer. What he desperately hoped was that Hench would be reasonable. Make allowances for a woman. But if he didn't . . .

"Do you really think you can beat them both?" Bud Hart drawled sarcastically.

Paxton's mouth tasted as if it were full of straw. He couldn't even work up enough spit to wet his lips. "I could use help," he said hollowly, "but I don't suppose either of you want a piece of this fight."

"Uh-uh," Tyson grunted, looking straight ahead.

Paxton took a deep breath. "What about you, Hart? I've always treated you fair."

"That's because I'm quick," he replied glibly. "No, this is your trouble. We'll just stay out of it and see what happens."

Tyson shifted in the saddle. "I think you'd better do what the man says, Paxton. He's got a pair of aces standing pat and you're about to tap out. Savvy?"

"Sure." He swore softly, bitterly. "Just make sure you both *do* sit this dance out. That way, you've got nothing to lose."

"Agreed," Tyson replied.

Paxton nudged his horse into a trot. He felt strung out tighter than a wire. Win or lose, he wanted to get this over in a hurry. Maybe he was wrong. Maybe Hench would let him keep Magdalena. But, deep inside, he knew that was a fool's hope. So he began to weigh every possible chance he had to survive. If he hoped to live through the next five minutes, he was going to have to be smart enough to come up with something damned quick. If he failed, the game would be over before it began. It was too bad Magdalena was still out cold; either way, she'd be mighty proud of him. She'd know she was loved by a man.

Paxton reined his horse in and dismounted before a word was spoken. He lifted his woman from the saddle and carried her by Hightower. He could feel Hench's eyes burning into him. Rio tried to block his path but he managed to step around and keep moving.

"Paxton!"

He kept walking toward the house. There was one chance, and that was that they wouldn't shoot him in the back carrying a girl in his arms.

"Paxton! Where the hell are you going?" Hench shouted.

"Into the house," he replied. "The girl is hurt. She needs to be taken care of."

"Stop! Turn around!"

He was on the porch, reaching for the door. His hand wavered, then grabbed the knob and he kicked it open. They were going to back-shoot him; he tensed, expecting a bullet. Maybe a backful that would throw him face first to die on a Persian rug.

Then, the door slammed shut behind and a flood of relief made his legs wobbly. He'd made it! There was a chance. Out in the yard, he'd instinctively realized there had been none. Rio and Chesterton would have separated in opposite directions and he'd have been caught from both sides with Hightower up front. But now, they'd have to come inside and stay close.

Paxton hurried toward a side bedroom. The house was dark and cool the way the old man liked it. But they'd have to come in together and they'd be a solid target. There was one other advantage, small, but, at this point, even a small advantage was important. Each moment that passed, his own eyes were becoming accustomed to the gloom. Both Rio and Chesterton would be coming in from bright sunlight and their vision would be faulty.

He gently placed Magdalena down on the bed and stared at her for a long moment. He thought he heard Hightower's voice shouting at him from outside but he ignored the distraction.

"I hope you know what I'm going to do for you, Magdalena," he whispered. "I reckon this makes us even for my killing your dad."

He unholstered his gun and checked it carefully. "I'd say if I pull us through you'll owe me your life and everything."

Paxton eased his six gun back into the holster and turned around knowing one thing—if he had to die, he was going to take the old man along, too.

Back inside the main room, he selected a position near the fireplace and waited. He knew Hightower well enough to be sure the rancher wouldn't be long in arriving; patience wasn't in the old man's blood.

Outside, everything was quiet. As quiet as sunset on a cemetery.

"Paxton! Paxton, we're coming in. I want to talk to you."

"Come on then!" he shouted.

The form of Hench Hightower silhouetted against the doorway. He's an easy target, Paxton thought, blinking in the sun and probably more scared of dying than I am.

For an instant, he almost drew and fired. He could have killed Hench right where he stood. But there was a basic instinct for survival that made him wait. Because if he gunned down Hench in the doorway, every man in the place would see it and they'd never let him walk out alive. They'd burn the house down with him and Magdalena inside if that was what it took.

"Howdy," Paxton said quietly.

Hench nodded. "That girl is a witness. You were wrong to bring her back alive."

"I couldn't kill her, Hench."

"Then you should have let someone else do it."

"She's a woman!"

"She's Fenton's daughter." Hench smiled. "Remember? He's the man you shot. That girl would dance on your grave." There was a long pause before he spoke again. "And she'll have the chance soon if you don't come to your senses."

Paxton swallowed dryly. He saw Chesterton slip in beside Hench and drop his gun hand just over his holster. Where was Rio! He knew the answer at once. Rio was coming around through the back door. If he wasn't already in shooting position, he would be within the next minute. Chesterton blinked rapidly, his eyes opening and closing like traps. And Paxton saw his one chance slipping away—so, without warning—he drew.

It was no contest. Chesterton was caught flat-footed with nowhere to go. He tried and his gun was clearing leather when Paxton's bullet slapped him out of the doorway in a roar of gunpowder.

"Freeze, Hench!"

The rancher's hand was on his gun butt; his eyes were locked on the barrel of Paxton's smoking six gun. It was aimed right at his chest. Hench flung up his hands.

"Don't shoot!"

Paxton strode forward until he was nose to nose with Hightower, then he laughed in the man's face and yanked him around. "Rio is going to have one hell of a big surprise, isn't he? Tell him to throw his gun down or I'll use your decrepit body as a shield. Tell him that!"

"I will," Hench rattled. "He'll obey my order."

Rio must have heard the shot and he came in low and fast around the corner just where Paxton knew he would.

"Drop it!" Hench shouted.

He was a dark, sinister-looking man, and in the half light

of the hallway, he made a small, deadly target. Paxton wanted to fire at him, but didn't. He held the gun to Hench's temple and waited. Rio was probably plenty good enough to get a bullet by Hench and strike a vital part of the larger man, but Paxton tried not to think of that.

"Rio, it's over," Hench called, with desperation thick in his voice.

"Is that right, Paxton?"

He nodded. "I'm no fool. I can't beat all of you."

Rio hesitated for a moment, then slowly holstered his gun. Paxton grinned, pulled the gun away from the old man's head, and carefully measured Rio down his sight. But, just as he was about to pull the trigger, Hench knocked his arm in a desperate effort to break free. Paxton knew as he fired that he was off-target. It was the break Rio needed and he went for his gun.

He *was* fast! Paxton crouched and snapped off two more shots, but Rio was in action. A bullet whip-cracked by his head and exploded into a desk lamp. Paxton worked his gun faster than ever before. Through the smoke, he thought he saw his target stagger, then he heard Rio's body strike the oaken floor; his gun clattered. Relief flooded through Paxton like warm spring water. For insurance, he took a slow aim and pulled the trigger. His hammer fell on an empty cylinder. It had been that close!

"Damn you!" Hench roared.

Paxton whipped around with an empty gun and saw Hench dragging up his loaded one. There was no time for anything but to jump at Hightower. He did. The six-shooter roared as they collided and Paxton felt a bullet sear down his leg. Desperately, he grabbed for the gun, twisted it, and an instant later, another shot muffled between them.

Hench Hightower stiffened and then slumped to the floor —dead.

Paxton heard the drumming of footsteps on the porch. He snatched up Hench's gun and aimed for the doorway. Tyson and Hart froze, then lifted their hands.

For a long moment, no one said a word. Then Paxton gritted, "What do you want?"

Tyson and Hart both grinned as big as split melons. "Not a damn thing, *boss*," Tyson drawled.

Paxton nodded. "That's what I thought. Go outside and tell three or four of the boys to come in and drag these vermin out of *my* house."

His stomach was churning and his mouth felt dry. But as his eyes swept across the room, surveying the rich furniture, the bright Persian rugs, and heavy velvet draperies—the solid empire that was now his own—Paxton Bullock knew he'd never felt better in his life.

"Hold it!" he called to Tyson and Hart. They stopped at the doorway. They looked worried, even scared. Already they respected his power.

"I want you both to move out of the bunkhouse. You're taking Rio's and Chesterton's rooms. I'll hire two more men to take your places on the range." He smiled. "The men you're replacing thought they were fast and smart. They were neither. You'll be expected to do better for me. Is that clear?"

"Yes, sir," they echoed.

"Good," he replied amicably. "I'll be with Magdalena until she wakes. When she does, I want no dead men lying around to upset her."

Tyson glanced at his companion with a strange look on his face. But he quickly turned back. "You can count on us," he said eagerly.

"I know," Paxton called back over his shoulder, "that's why you're still alive."

CHAPTER 11

Darby Buckingham leaned closer to the campfire and peered intently at his young friend. "Tomorrow, I'm going to try to catch a mustang, even though I haven't the least idea of how to go about it. As you know, I am inept with a horse and totally incompetent with a rope."

But catch a horse he must. Darby knew it was out of the question to consider walking the sixty miles back to town. Jory had lost too much blood.

"There is one way," Jory said, "but I'm not sure it would work."

"Let's hear it," Darby said quickly.

"Are you any good with a rifle?"

Darby almost laughed outright.

"That's what I was afraid of. You see, I've heard that it's possible to nick a mustang. You aim to crease it along the top of the neck, right in front of the withers and close to the spinal column. If it's done just right—and I mean perfectly—they say the bullet will stun the mustang."

Darby scowled. "And if it isn't?"

"You either miss entirely or you kill a horse," Jory said flatly. He stared into the fire a long time. "Jerome Jerome probably could have done it one out of three or four times. I've seen Paxton try again and again. He's a pretty fair shot but there are a lot of dead horses that wouldn't think so."

"Then let's pass on the creasing idea," Darby said gruffly. "Neither one of us came here to kill mustangs. Surely, there must be other ways a single man can try."

"Oh yeah, there are," Jory said. "The best one I've ever

seen is where a fella locates a water hole, then builds a corral around it. Doesn't have to be big."

"I could do that," Darby said quickly. "Then what?"

"Then he goes around to every other watering hole and plants a 'spook.'"

"What's that?"

"Oh, could be a piece of cloth hanging from a nearby tree, or even digging up a few clumps of sagebrush and piling them in front of the water holes with a couple of rocks on top. Anything that is unnatural will scare a herd and keep them away."

Darby nodded with interest. "I see. The spooks keep the horses away from every water hole but one—the one with the corral. Sooner or later, they have to come down and drink."

"That's right," Jory nodded, "the only trouble is that a man on foot could never find all the water holes within, say, twenty miles. If you miss even one, the whole plan fails."

"Blast!" Darby swore in frustration.

"There are plenty of ways a lone mustanger can catch horses. Take Maggie's father, for instance. Fenton believed the best way was to hide near a watering place, wait until the horses had drunk their fill, and then go after them with a long rope."

A faint smile touched Jory's lips. "You should have seen them. I went along a couple of times and just watched. He and Maggie would strip off their saddles, tie ropes around their horses' necks, and charge those mustangs just as they finished drinking. A waterlogged horse can't go more than a mile at a hard run. It hurts them too much. Fenton and Maggie would take their pick and rope the best. By dropping that extra saddle weight, they could catch the fastest mustang on the range providing it had just satisfied its thirst. Once the loop settled, they'd start reining in, gradually cutting off the mustang's wind until it tumbled down with exhaustion."

Jory shook his head in wonder. "When Fenton was feel-

ing especially good, he'd get fancy and throw the slack over
the mustang's quarters and hind legs. Then he'd turn his
horse at a right angle, and when the slack came up tight, the
wild horse would flip down hard. It took the fight out of the
meanest stallion. Busted like that and waterlogged to boot,
Fenton would have their front and back hoofs tied up and
go after another without even breathing hard."

"I wish I could have seen them," Darby said.

"Well, perhaps Maggie will . . ." His voice trailed off and
he stared at the fire for several minutes again before speaking. "We don't need horse stories now," he said at last. "But
a man on foot and alone, even a real mustanger, wouldn't
have an easy time catching a horse."

"I'm not looking for an *easy* way to anything, Jory. Just
come up with something I can at least try! If, after three or
four days, I fail, then we're going to have to start walking."

Jory nodded. "There are a few things you could do that
might work, given a little luck."

"Then let's hear them," Darby said. "Anything is better
than walking sixty miles."

"The only way you can get close enough to a mustang is
to surprise him when he goes down to drink. I've heard stories of a man named Mustang Grey whose horse broke a leg
and stranded him a long ways from help. The way the story
goes, Grey located a water hole where mustangs came.
Then he climbed up into a tree and dropped a loop over one
as they passed by. It seems reasonable, because the scent of
a man, or a cougar for that matter, doesn't seem to float
down. That's why they always drop from up above."

Darby swallowed hard. "I might have to wait in a tree for
days."

"Not likely," Jory replied. "Mustangs always follow a
schedule, just like people. Usually, they either water at dusk
or dawn. Take your pick and be ready."

Darby thought it over. He couldn't quite picture himself
perched in a tree all day. He wasn't even sure he could
climb one.

"There must be another way," he said hopefully.

"Only one other I know of."

"Don't tell me," Darby grunted cryptically. "They pass through the opening of a narrow canyon, and I leap off the rim. But the horse happens to see me falling and moves. When I splatter, anything left of me is trampled by the others and that's the end of the story."

Jory laughed, but grimaced at his wound and eyed his friend with amusement. "It's not quite that bad. I was thinking you could try a foot trap."

"Go on," Darby urged. This sounded good already.

"It's pretty simple. You find a horse trail to water. Then, during the middle of the day, you dig a little hole and bury a loop about an inch under the dirt, right in the center of the path. For yourself, you dig another hole nearby. When the mustangs trail in, one steps in the loop and you yank up the slack. Then he's all yours."

"Humph," Darby grunted in an approving tone, "it might work."

"It will if you're careful to leave no signs for them to see. You have to brush over your tracks, cover the rope, and pull some mesquite over your nest to keep the mustangs from catching your scent."

"I'll give it a try."

"It's your choice, but I'd first take a whirl at loopin' one from a tree," Jory said seriously. "It's a whole lot less work and you could have one by tomorrow night or the day after. But if you have to scout all the horse trails, dig a big hole, and cart fresh dirt off somewhere, it's going to take longer."

"Hmm. I hadn't thought of that," Darby admitted.

He dug one of the few cigars he had left out of his saddle-bags. He was willing to try anything to hasten their return to Elko. There was no telling what was going on with Maggie. And though he was sure Paxton must have had some purpose for sparing the girl, the purpose that came to mind was not comforting. He hoped Jory was not harboring the same dark thoughts. But until they reached town and got help from the doctor and the sheriff, there wasn't a damned thing he could do.

There was one other possibility that had him worried and that was the chance that a Hightower rider might spot them and report back to headquarters. If that happened, their fates were as good as sealed. So he brooded quietly over his cigar until the hour grew late and Jory slept well. Mustangs were easy enough to track to the river. All he had to do was locate a spot where they filed down to drink, then find an overhanging tree and figure out a way to climb the blasted thing. Then, as they passed underneath, drop the loop through the branches and hope it caught a mustang.

He scowled. What then? How would he manage to subdue the beast? His recent experiences suggested that he was ill suited for breaking a horse. There were bruises all over his body testifying their savagery and his incompetence.

Darby tossed his cigar onto the coals and climbed into his bedroll. He surveyed the stars above and wondered what was going to happen tomorrow. His instincts warned that the tree-catch method was going to be futile if not disastrous. But, for the sake of expediency, he'd give it at least one try. If it failed, he had no intention of perching on a limb for days until something blundered along. With the foot trap, at least one could wait in comfort without fear of plunging off the bough of a tree and breaking one's neck.

Darby was feeling very satisfied with himself. Immensely satisfied. Twenty feet above a cleft in the riverbank, there could be no mistake that he was in a perfect spot from which to drop his loop. The limb upon which he was straddled was almost as thick as his leg. Darby leaned contentedly against the trunk and enjoyed a fine late afternoon breeze and an excellent view of the sun diving toward the Tuscaroras. He was almost directly above the river and noted with pleasure the occasional rippling splashes as big trout jumped for bugs that showed no indication of wanting to fly up and bother him. If he'd been able to light a cigar, and if a particularly aggressive type of tree ant had been less inclined to bite, he decided that the branch of a spreading cottonwood tree would not be a bad place at all.

Still, despite the pleasantness of his surroundings, he was impatient for the mustangs to arrive. In the mud below, there was an abundance of fresh tracks and droppings that left no doubt that this was a well-frequented watering spot.

Across his knees, the loop was ready. He'd taken Jory's advice and tied the end around the branch in a sort of half hitch that could be quickly pulled free. The reason for the half hitch was that he didn't want to risk choking the horse to death if it fell or somehow got tangled in the brush or with another of the band. If either of those things occurred, he'd be able to release the knot quickly and perhaps hobble the beast before it recovered.

In respect to what animal he should rope, Jory had been adamant that it not be the stallion. A man on foot would have little chance of gentling one and would probably end up being stomped to death or flying back up the tree. Jory's advice had been that he pick a smaller mare and one that looked reasonably levelheaded. That levelheaded business was the hard part. Jory hadn't been able to explain how one could tell one type from another. He'd just said that after a man was around mustangs long enough he could tell by the way they looked. Darby would just have to take his chances and hope his luck held. And so far, so good.

The sun dipped behind the mountains and the river grew black as the trout gave up on catching dinner. Darby's empty stomach rumbled and his body grew stiff from the vigil. But something held him still. This was dusk. The fleeting time between day and night. The time when Jory said mustangs came to drink.

He twisted around and almost fell off his branch. There they were! Darby ignored the biting ants, forgot the cold and his own hunger.

Though he'd been careful to circle around the trail, and he'd brushed his tracks away, Darby was still worried. But, as the stallion led his band closer, there was no indication that he scented man or felt any danger. As they approached the cut in the bank, Darby saw them file in one behind another in what he supposed was some kind of rough pecking order.

The stallion appeared to be either black or bay; he couldn't tell for sure in the fading light. It was a small herd, less than ten mares and two or three foals. The stallion's muzzle was almost dusting the trail as he pranced forward.

But then he was passing underneath the tree and Darby's hands felt sticky on the loop as he edged it away from his body. It was impossible now to tell which of the animals below appeared sensible or crazy. And Darby didn't care. All that mattered was that the loop passed down without catching on a low branch and found its mark.

He leaned forward as far as he dared. The stallion was drinking; some of the mares were starting to lower their heads to the water. Darby's outstretched arms guided the loop to outline a mustang directly below.

He dropped the rope.

The loop fell perfectly. The moment the rope touched her body, the mare's head snapped up and Darby saw the lasso tighten under her jaw and around the top of her neck. In the same instant, everything below exploded as the horses leapt in all directions. Some jumped right into the river and others slammed into the bank, trees, and shrubs in a panic to escape. Darby didn't see all this but that was his general impression and he was immensely grateful he wasn't down there. His victim jumped, too. She hit the end of the rope, and twenty feet above, the big limb bent sideways, creaking in protest. Darby tottered, almost fell, but managed to get both arms around the limb and he hugged it tightly.

The lassoed mare went absolutely crazy, pitching and throwing herself in every direction. Each time she hit the end of the rope, she flipped over or screamed. After the first few seconds, Darby saw he had a big problem. The beast was throttling herself to death. The mare's eyes were rolling upward at him and she was leaning her full weight against the rope with all four hoofs ripping up great hunks of river bed in a desperate effort to break away. The animal's tongue lolled out and Darby could hear her throat squeezing shut.

There was no time to think. He needed that horse alive, not dead. Darby yanked the half hitch loose. With no thought of life or limb, he grabbed the rope end in one hand and jumped.

His approach from above must have pushed the mare over the edge of insanity. He was still in mid-air when she flipped over backward. Dimly, he felt himself being yanked sideways in a violent motion. And, instead of landing on soil, he was catapulted into the river. But he hung on.

He hung on even when the demented creature began dragging him through the mud and rocks as she galloped down the riverbank. He hung on when the heavy willows and slime covered his eyes, nose, and mouth until he couldn't breathe. He let go only when he hit a half-submerged stump and felt his arms almost pop out of his shoulders.

Darby lay in the water a long time, struggling to force his body to move. And when it finally did, it was merely to roll deeper into the water to wash away the clotting muck and numb his pain.

"All right," Jory said, "so I was wrong about the tree idea. Maybe there never was a man called Mustang Grey. All I know is that's the story."

"Let *me* make up the stories after this," Darby gritted. "Now, are you sure you've told me *everything* you can about the foot trap? Has it really been tested?"

Jory's expression grew hangdog. "Of course," he muttered. "What happened last night won't happen again."

"I couldn't survive it a second time," Darby growled.

The next day, Darby managed to push the debacle out of his mind and concentrate on the foot trap. Now, as he crouched in what Jory called a nest and waited, he reviewed his work, trying to think of anything he might have forgotten. The circular hole in the trail was about a yard wide and only two feet deep. Just below the surface, he'd patched a floor of sticks and settled the loop in very carefully. Then he'd covered the hole until it was level with the trail. The rope was buried all the way to his nest. The idea was that a horse would unwittingly put a foot into the trap, breaking the sticks loudly enough for him to know when to yank. Jory said it usually worked.

There was another thing that was going to work better this time, and that was a slight refinement in the way the roped horse was to be controlled. For, as strong as he was, Darby knew it was ridiculous to try and match muscle with a wild horse. So this time, he had a log positioned just in front of his nest with the rope tied to one end. After he had sprung the foot trap, he would let go of the rope and let the log serve as an anchor. It wasn't a large piece of wood, but big enough that, after a horse dragged it around for five or ten minutes, the animal would be exhausted. Then, while the beast stood panting with its head down between its legs, Darby would try to become its friend. Jory and he had agreed that he would be better off trying to return immediately to camp. There, at least, Jory could watch and give suggestions and the mustang would be in the corral.

But he didn't even want to think about that now. He'd been hiding in the hole since early afternoon and he was tired of being doubled up in a ball like a rodent in its burrow. In the tree, he had had a view and some fresh air! But after six hours of crouching and staring at a dirt wall, Darby reckoned he knew what real boredom was. He tried to make the time go faster by thinking about his book on Nevada mustangs. In fact, he was just wishing he'd brought a pen and some paper when he heard a wild horse bugling from the hillside.

Darby rose until his head was touching the uprooted sagebrush he'd piled over his hole. And, in the dusky light, he saw them coming. He eased back into his nest and let the minutes drag by. But, when he heard a nicker, he knew they were close.

Moments later, the sticks broke and he was somehow surprised. It was more a reflex action than anything else that made him jerk. In less than a second, the rope yanked taut and his log vanished.

This was it!

He tried to jump to his feet and found himself sprawling in the dirt with a pair of legs that had fallen asleep.

There were horses going in every direction. But the only one Darby watched was a big, gangly roan with a lasso around its fetlock and murder in its rolling eyes. The horse had already dragged the log fifty yards by the time Darby, cursing and slapping his legs to promote circulation, began to stump his way after it.

The sight of him seemed to renew the animal in its quest for freedom and Darby slowed his steps and watched with growing fear that the mustang would break a leg.

"Easy," he crooned. Darby walked slowly over to the log. The horse pivoted, its left foreleg suspended outward by the rope. The animal's eyes were wild and its nostrils expanded and contracted rapidly with its breathing. But at least, Darby thought, its ears are pointing forward rather than lying back. He grasped the rope and started toward the horse.

The mustang tried to whirl, and on three legs, it lost balance and crashed to the dirt, thrashing at the rope and surrounding brush. This was exactly what Darby wanted. He rushed forward, drawing a pair of hobbles from his pocket. He had just finished putting them on the front legs, as Jory had instructed him, when the roan bit him in the back.

Never, never in his life had he known such pain to exist!

Hobbles forgotten, Darby let out a bellow that might have awakened the sleeping children in Elko, more than sixty miles away. The beast hung onto his flesh, and when he finally managed to tear himself out of its grip, the roan's teeth clicked together like the jaws of a bear trap.

It was a good twenty minutes before he knew he could trust himself near the mustang. He wanted to strangle it and was sure he could. But finally, his black anger cooled and he was able to view the horse more rationally. After all, it didn't bite out of meanness, did it? He hoped not, and as he began to gather some firewood and cook something to eat, he passed by the roan several times, trying to read the intent in the expanded whites of her rolling eyes.

He warmed some water and made tea and he burned some dried meat and ate it from the frying pan. The food wasn't good but it did fill him and he was always much more charitable on a full stomach.

"Horse," he said, "tonight you and I have to reach an agreement. In the morning, you are going to accompany me back to Jory and, later in the day, allow me to ride you. In return for your co-operation, you'll be released as soon as we reach town."

He moved closer, until he could touch the horse's neck. "Come now, I'd say that was more than fair. Wouldn't you?"

The teeth missed his hand by less than an inch and rattled his composure. "Now listen," Darby said shakily, "if I have to talk with you all night, I will. Because in the morning, we leave together! I'm here to improve your lot, though you're probably not aware of it. And I've seen the ways men lead you away from this country. Now don't make me do that, because if it boils down to a choice of inflicting painful measures on you, or wasting days out here when Maggie needs us, then you lose, horse."

Again the roan snapped, but this time Darby had no illusions as to its real nature. He dodged the teeth and sat down on its neck in a way that entirely prevented any more foolishness.

"Tonight," he said, reaching for a cigar, "I'm going to recite some Shakespeare and Milton. I'll select compas-

sionate poems that will soothe your wicked soul. And I trust
that when the sun rises, we'll be friends."

The roan was almost docile by morning, but Darby took
no chances and left the hobbles on its front legs. Before full
daylight, he was leading the mare out of the valley and talking to her as if she were an old friend. He wasn't a man to
hold grudges, even though a patch of purple skin stood up
on his back. Besides that, in a few hours he would have to
try to ride the big roan. It seemed more than prudent, given
his less than competent riding ability, to try to get on good
terms with the horse.

Jory yelled through the fence, "Don't yank the blindfold
off until you're up! And don't let go of her ear until you're
ready."

Darby swallowed dryly. He'd elected to try and break the
roan fast. There were easier ways, but they were much
slower. Like spending hours stepping into the stirrup and
gradually increasing body weight until the mustang grew
accustomed to it and probably wouldn't buck at all. But, as
much as he would have liked to do it that way, there just
wasn't time. Darby managed to get his boot to the stirrup of
old Jerome Jerome's saddle. But with his left hand locked on
the roan's ear and his right hand around the saddle horn, it
was going to be tricky getting up—much less staying on.

Well, there's no sense in prolonging it, he thought fatalis-
tically. With a heave, he pulled himself off the ground and
whipped his leg over the saddle.

"Turn her loose!" Jory yelled.

He did. Darby released the ear, pulled the blindfold, and
grabbed for the saddle horn with both hands as the mustang
lowered its back, then suddenly arched toward the sky,
squealing all the way up and down again. The roan landed
stiff-legged, with all four hoofs close together. Darby felt as
if he had earthquakes in his innards. His shoulders seemed
to be yanked down over his ribs and, when the horse shot
back up in the air, his neck snapped his eyes skyward. The

roan crashed to the ground harder than the first time and Darby felt the strength go out of his back.

"Yee-haw! Ride him, Darby!"

Suddenly, the roan twisted sideways like a snake and Darby found himself hitting the ground on his feet, then flipping into the rails.

"I don't believe it!" he gasped. "I'll never ride her in a hundred years."

"Good ride," Jory called. "You'll do better next time."

He didn't want a next time—ever. But he didn't say that. Instead, he walked over to the roan, which waited for him with what he swore was a disdainful expression.

They did it all over again. Four times. And at the end, when Darby was drunkenly weaving around in circles with a bloody nose, Jory stepped into the corral and caught him by the arm. "You've had enough," he said grimly. "It's my turn."

"No!" Darby realized he'd shouted. "If you ride, your wound will open and you could bleed to death."

Jory swore. "You've got the worst kind of bronc there is— a damn pile driver. She'll shake something loose inside you pretty soon."

"So what can I do?" he gasped.

"Tie a saddle roll behind the horn and wedge yourself in. Those buckskins . . . we'll wet them so they grip the seat of the saddle instead of slide. Finally, tie the stirrups together under her belly. That way, you'll have more leg control." Jory's face was grim. "But, if that isn't enough, then we'll tie her foreleg up and see how she bucks on three legs."

"Why," Darby asked weakly, "didn't you suggest these measures from the beginning?"

Jory avoided his eyes. "I guess I figured if you were going to write about bronc bustin', you had to have done it."

Ordinarily, under similar conditions, Darby Buckingham would have exploded. But there was just nothing left to waste on the kid. Every ounce of strength and anger he had, he directed at the roan. He whirled away, intent on getting his bedroll tied behind the fork of that saddle. And, while he was doing it, he'd wet the buckskins.

The roan watched him return. It was caked with sweat and white foam. For the first time, Darby felt hope. At least the creature was having to exert itself. He tied the bedroll in place and the mustang waited patiently. It seemed to realize nothing would occur until he was seated. They'd dispensed with the ear lock and blindfold three unloadings ago.

Darby jammed his boot into the stirrup and swung aboard. And, just like every time before, the roan arced and launched itself as if it were trying to bite the clouds. They came down hard . . . but not as hard. His head, as before, snapped back and forth each time they struck the earth, but not as sharply, and it seemed that his buckskins clung to the saddle as though they were glued. Maybe, too, it was the bedroll that he'd wedged in place. But whatever, this time, when the roan finally dodged sideways, Darby stayed right along with her.

He might have been the most surprised one of them all. It gave him life and he let loose of the horn with one hand and extended it for balance. But the roan didn't quit easily. It seemed to take forever to Darby but, dimly, he knew she was finished. Maybe he did cheat, a little, but he didn't care. He wiped his face with the back of a leather sleeve and, when the roan began to hop rather than buck, he smiled.

"Yee-haw!" Jory howled. "You did it!"

He nodded, too weak to answer, while the roan carried him around and around inside the corral as peaceably as a stable horse.

CHAPTER 12

They reached Elko in three days and Darby walked most of the sixty miles. When he entered town, no one recognized him as the Easterner who'd departed less than two months earlier. The same clothes were on his back, yet they no longer fit tightly about the waist, only in the shoulders, chest, and arms. Instead of his former solid block, Darby's new proportions were wedge-shaped, lean, and rugged.

He matched the stares of those who gawked until they looked away. Darby was in a black mood. There had been four of them who had ridden out the last time—now it was just he and Jory Parnes. His first stop was going to be the sheriff's office. And if the man didn't want to co-operate, he guessed he'd probably have to rough him up a little. There was obviously no respect for the law in Elko County, and there wasn't any reason to set a precedent. But, like it or not, Sheriff John Salton was going to ride out to see Hench Hightower just as soon as Jory had been to a doctor and they bought some more ammunition.

They'd bring Maggie back if she was on Hench's ranch. He wasn't sure how, but they'd do it if it meant going through Paxton Bullock and his whole crowd.

Darby said it plainly one more time. "You're the sheriff. I demand you accompany us to search for the missing girl."

"Now, now," Salton replied placatingly, "take it easy. You say it had to be Mr. Hightower's boys who ambushed you. Do you have any proof?"

"Proof!" Darby exploded. "Who else would want us all dead?"

The sheriff was a narrow-shouldered, hollow-cheeked man with a small nose, a weak chin, and a blustery voice. He was only a little taller than Darby but probably weighed eighty pounds less. Darby noted with disdain that his biceps were no thicker than a normal pair of wrists. And, from his protestations, Darby had a hunch his courage matched his insignificant appearance. The man apparently lacked both character and substance. How he'd ever gotten elected was a mystery.

The sheriff walked across his office and turned, jabbing a finger at Darby. "How am I supposed to know who your enemies are?" His eyes narrowed and a threatening tone crept into his voice. "We were doin' fine until you showed up in Elko, mister. You went around shooting off your mouth about how Mr. Hightower operated. Well, there are a lot of people who owe him favors and don't like strangers stirring up accusations and such. And any of his friends could have shot at your group."

"You don't have the nerve," Darby graveled, "and I'm beginning to suspect you're Hightower's only supporter. How many votes can one man control?"

"Gawddamn you! I won't stand for talk like that!"

"And I won't stand for your lack of initiative. Like it or not, Sheriff, you are taking a ride out to Hightower's with Jory and me within the hour. And if we find the girl being held, you're going to arrest Hench and jail the man for murder and abduction."

"And if I refuse?"

Darby's fists clenched menacingly. "We're alone and I'm in no mood for refusal. One way or the other, you'll come."

The sheriff's mouth opened, then snapped shut in white-lipped fury. His gun hand strayed toward his holster. But he never followed up the threat and Darby waited, as impassive as a cigar-store Indian.

Even though John Salton was the most pathetic example of a sheriff Darby had ever encountered, he was the law. Hightower would think twice before he acted rashly. He still might. But if so, Darby wanted Salton to know he was going to be right in the center when bullets started flying.

"Oh, Mr. Buckingham!"

Both he and the sheriff spun around to see the editor, Jim Plankton, charge into the office.

"What do you want?" the sheriff demanded in a tone that clearly indicated they were enemies.

"Why, a story, of course," Plankton beamed. "Mr. Buckingham's story. The whole town is waiting to hear the news."

"He hasn't got time," came the officious reply. "We've got to ride."

"Where to?"

"Plankton. This is law business!"

"It's also news." Plankton yanked a pad free and began to scribble. "Please, Mr. Buckingham, you can tell me while you prepare to leave. The people of this town have a right to know what is going on here."

The man was correct about that, Darby thought. And, just as importantly, perhaps a story would give the sheriff some concern for his own future if he sided completely with Hightower. There was no telling what was going to happen, but Darby knew full well the power of a printing press when it came to truth and justice. So, right then, he decided to give Plankton a story that would sell papers all the way from Carson City to Denver, Colorado. It wouldn't take long. Less time than it required for the doctor to examine Jory Parnes.

"All right," Darby said, secretly enjoying the stricken look that appeared on John Salton's face. "I guess you do need a story. Seven days ago, Jerome Jerome was blown out of his saddle by an ambusher's bullet and a young girl whom the town knows well had her horse shot out from under her and was then abducted."

"Terrific," Plankton breathed, "what a story! Don't stop now."

"I'm only getting started, but I'll have to cut it a little

shorter than I'd like. We're on our way to find the girl. Sheriff Salton agrees with me that the Hightower Ranch is the most obvious place to start."

Plankton stopped writing. He frowned up at Darby. "Aw, come on."

"Write it!" Salton yelled. "Every word."

The editor removed his glasses, thoughtfully wiped them on his vest, and blinked up at Darby. "Okay, I'll write it," he said wearily, "but he's not fooling me."

"Just say," Darby continued, "we won't rest until we've found Magdalena Lamesa."

Jory Parnes walked in and Darby's attention was immediately fixed on the young man. "What did the doctor say?"

"He said you should have been in medicine instead of a writer. I've got three cracked ribs on the right side where the bullet passed. Other than that, the rest is fine."

Jory patted the Smith & Wesson that rested behind his belt. "While you were out catching that mustang, I was practicing again."

"Can you draw with three broken ribs?" the sheriff asked.

Jory raised his right hand and said, "Slowly. Very slowly."

That pleased Darby because, without actually lying, he'd given the sheriff the impression he would draw and shoot right-handed. The man had just naturally assumed he would, and Jory was smart enough to let him think so. Darby hoped that Paxton Bullock would reach the same conclusion. In the sheriff's case, however, it wasn't that he distrusted Salton enough to think he'd take sides, but Jory's draw was going to be remembered, and the first time he pulled iron with his left hand, he'd have an edge. Darby had a feeling they'd need that edge very badly against Paxton Bullock.

"Let's ride," Darby said, and they started to leave.

"Wait a minute!" He turned and the editor almost crashed into him. "I want to go along."

"No," Salton snapped.

"Yes," Darby countered. "If you're aware that there might be trouble."

The editor pulled back his coat to show that he was armed. "In the West, the mortality rate among newspaper writers and editors is very high. A prudent journalist, such as myself, believes it just as important to sharpen one's marksmanship as one's wordsmanship, if you follow my reasoning."

"Of course," Darby said, with a trace of amusement lifting the corners of his mouth. "You're saying you want to live to write the truth no matter who disputes your opinion. I like that and welcome your company."

Darby glanced over at John Salton; he looked mad. Jory's expression was one of worried anticipation and the editor showed eager expectancy on every line of his face.

"Let's go find Magdalena Lamesa," Darby said. "I don't have much doubt where we'll locate her."

"You'd better let me ride in first," the sheriff cautioned as he wiped his face nervously.

"Sounds reasonable," Darby replied, "but we'll be right behind you." He glanced over at Jory, then at Plankton. "The idea is to rescue Magdalena, not engage the entire Hightower Ranch in a gun battle that could only result in our deaths."

"If he's got Maggie," Jory said, his voice tight, "I'm not leaving without her. No matter what happens."

"Listen to me," Darby growled, "if she's there, we'll find a way to get her. But not now. It is absolutely pointless to die in a vain and stupid attempt at force. There are other ways!"

It was a long moment before Jory nodded stiffly. "You're right, damn it. Neither of us can help her if we're shot. It was bad enough for her dad and then Jerome Jerome."

"Very true. All right. Let's go in and see Mr. Hightower."

As they rode closer, Darby saw at least twenty men assemble outside the ranch house, but not one of them was the rancher himself. Instead, they seemed to be gathering around a big and familiar form whom Darby knew very well —Paxton Bullock. Darby cradled a shotgun across his lap. He figured there was a very good chance he'd have to use it. His advice to Jory had been based on the decidedly optimistic assumption that Hench and Paxton would allow them to leave. If there was any chance at all, it was that the editor and sheriff were witnesses.

"Far enough!" Paxton called. Up ahead, the sheriff yanked hard on the reins and Darby walked his horse right by the man until he was less than ten feet from Paxton with Jory almost touching him, stirrup to stirrup.

"Where's Hightower?" Darby demanded. "What I've got to say is for him."

A thin smile crossed Paxton's lips. He glanced toward two men beside him and the smile grew wider. "I'm afraid," he drawled, "you're out of luck. Yes, sir, your luck has just ended, Buckingham. You see, Hench had a little accident. Two of his men, Rio and Chesterton, got into an argument and damned if poor ol' Hench didn't catch a bullet. Rio's, I think, though it don't matter because I shot him for what he done to the boss, and Chesterton was already dead."

The sheriff whistled softly. "No witnesses? None at all?" he asked bleakly.

"Just me," said Paxton. "And before the old man died, he gave the whole spread to yours truly. He had a real soft spot for me. Almost like as if I was his son. Ain't that right, Jory?"

"You're lying to your toes," Jory said harshly. "Mr. Hightower didn't trust anyone. Least of all you."

Paxton stiffened and his eyelids dropped. "I see you're packing a gun, Jory. I reckon you'd better step down and use it."

Jory started to dismount but Darby's words stopped him. "We've come for the girl, Paxton, not trouble."

"Yeah. Where is she?" Jory almost shouted.

"What girl?"

"Magdalena Lamesa," Darby said.

Paxton shrugged. "I don't know anything about her. Sorry."

Jim Plankton's voice was hard. "Sheriff, there's an easy way to find out. Let's search the house."

"Oh no," Paxton warned.

"Sheriff, this whole thing is mighty suspicious and my readers are going to be damned skeptical about Hench's death and the girl's disappearance. Unless you and I are allowed to search that house right now, I'm going to write the U.S. marshal and explain the circumstances. I'm sure *he* won't be afraid to seek the answer."

The editor jumped about a hundred points in Darby's estimation and he'd already been high. Now, with some amusement, he watched the struggle going on behind Paxton's eyes. The sheriff looked absolutely exasperated. Maybe he was coming up for re-election or perhaps he'd been a real friend of the deceased. Whatever, it was clear he didn't like the way things were going and couldn't figure a way out. Not with Plankton ready to fill his newspaper with less than encouraging commentary and speculation.

"Paxton, I had better take a look inside," the sheriff said hesitantly. "No offense, but if what you said about the girl is true, there's no sense in your raising a fuss."

"Damnit!" Paxton's face darkened. He turned around for a moment, obviously not worried about anyone shooting him. Maybe it was because of the two gunmen, but he sure wasn't concerned. Darby guessed that was his measure of confidence.

After a minute, he pivoted on his boot heels. His hand lifted to scratch his head as though he were puzzled about something. "What did you say the girl's name was?"

"Maggie Lamesa!" Jory swore. "You know damn well who she is."

Paxton chuckled, then knocked the side of his head roughly with his knuckles. "Why, I don't know what's the matter with me." He grinned. "To be perfectly honest, she's inside. Probably sleepin', though. You see, we found her out on the range all busted up from a horse fall. She broke her shoulder but we've been doctorin' her real good."

Paxton scuffed his toe around in the dirt. "Fact is, Maggie and I have sorta been spending a lot of time together since Hench died and we found her." Paxton looked right into Jory's eyes and laughed. It was a clever, calculating move to get Jory to draw and Darby knew it was going to work. Without thinking about it, Darby shot a straight right hand at Jory and felt his knuckles connect on the side of the younger man's jaw. Jory slumped forward, out cold, and Darby managed to catch him by the shirt and keep him from falling.

Paxton shook his head. "He's kinda fun to hit, ain't he?"

But Darby wasn't going for it, even though his stomach churned with anger. "We're not leaving until we talk to Magdalena," he graveled.

"All right. But you'll have to wait awhile out here until I get her out of bed." He grinned. "She might not be dressed for company."

"Just get her!" Darby hissed between clenched teeth.

Maggie heard the footsteps she'd grown to dread. They were heavy strides and, on the oak hallway to her room, they always grew faint just before reaching her door. Then, on tiptoe, Paxton would enter.

The first time he did, she tried to kill him. But it was hopeless. He'd warded off her blows until she couldn't swing any longer. Her shoulder hurt so badly, she'd gotten sick and the fight was over.

Since then, he was around her constantly. He'd never touched her—not yet. But his eyes seemed to burn with a strange and fierce glow and she was more scared of Paxton Bullock than if he'd said he was going to kill her. And though she didn't want to admit it, she knew why she was alive, there was just something in those eyes that told her better than words.

This time, when he unlocked the windowless room, she

sensed something was wrong. "Maggie," he whispered, striding over to the bed, "you've got to help me."

She shook her head.

"You'd better! 'Cause if you don't, I'm going to kill a couple of folks out there. And their names are Parnes and Buckingham!" She took a sharp breath and he laughed. "So, you've changed your mind, have you?"

"Yes, damn it!"

"I thought you might, my dear. I want you to come outside in your nightgown and tell them you want to stay."

He had to be crazy! She couldn't do it.

As though he read her mind, Paxton turned back to the door. "Very well," he said over his shoulder, "your choice. If necessary, I'll kill them all."

"Wait!"

"Yes?" he asked with a smile.

He'd beaten her and there was nothing she could do. She wanted to cry or to scream and yet neither would make a bit of difference to this man. "What do you want?" she pleaded.

Quickly, he strode over to her and she willed her hand not to draw back when his own covered it.

"Magdalena. I want *you*."

Maybe he saw something change in her expression, because she felt his hand tighten until her eyes widened in pain.

"Not like that. Not yet, anyway. You're different. You're my woman. I knew it the instant I saw you up there on the mountain. And I saved your life. Me! I did it for you."

She nodded, swallowing hard. Not understanding, but not daring to show it.

"I want you to . . . to be my woman always," he said thickly. "And to prove it, I'll let those two ride out alive if you'll just give me a chance and stop hating. That's all I ask in exchange for their lives! Will you do it?"

"Yes! Yes. Yes," she whispered. "Just don't kill them."

"I won't. You'll be there to see them go." He reached down and slipped a muscular arm under her back.

"I can walk!"

"I know," he said, his face inches from her own. "I just want to make sure they get the right impression."

Darby saw Paxton carrying her out and he felt his insides tighten. Clearly, Paxton had a perfect shield if anyone started shooting. Maggie looked pale. Darby squeezed the saddle horn and glanced down at Jory. It was a damned good thing he was out. This was more than enough to bear.

"Magdalena?" he asked. "Are you all right?"

She nodded. "My shoulder is hurt but it's going to be fine in a few weeks."

"You should come to town and see the doctor," Jim Plankton suggested.

"That's right," Darby said quickly, "we'll take you back now."

There was a shooting of pain across her face and Darby couldn't be sure, but he thought Paxton had squeezed her. Oh, he wanted that man!

"I . . . I don't think that's too good an idea," she said. "When I can ride without pain, I'll do that."

"She's enjoying her stay," Paxton said easily.

"Mr. Buckingham says these folks ambushed you," Sheriff Salton blurted. "I can see that ain't so." He shot a mean look at Darby.

"Must have been a mistake," Darby agreed. Reining his horse away from Maggie was the hardest thing he'd ever done in his life, yet he did it anyway. But first, he met her gaze and there was an unspoken understanding that passed between them. The words she spoke said one thing, her eyes said entirely the opposite.

"See you soon, Maggie."

"Good-by. Tell Jory . . . tell him I'm fine. Is he all right?"

"He will be. I had to put him to sleep for a few minutes lest he make a foolish and fatal mistake."

She nodded. "Just tell him I'm fine."

Darby led the way out. What was going to happen now? As long as Paxton ruled, nothing would change. And, with the girl in bondage, he knew full well that no one would make a move to break his dominance over this land.

Still, he thought he'd seen something strange in Paxton's way with Magdalena. Something that told him the man wasn't keeping her just for insurance. No, he'd seen a mixture of tenderness and lust that made Darby realize something had to be done quickly or the girl was lost.

The editor reined his horse in beside Darby's. "You really pack a wallop. Jory is still out cold."

"You know why I did that?"

"Sure. And so will he when he wakes. You saved all of our lives. I thank you, my wife and children thank you."

"Forget it," Darby mumbled.

"What are you going to do now?"

Darby noticed the sheriff was trying to act as though he wasn't listening. "We gave her a choice and she refused. Guess I was wrong."

"Good!" Salton said too quickly. "I'm glad to hear you're dropping those wild accusations and leaving Elko."

"I'm not."

"You're . . . you're staying? But why?"

"I still intend to catch horses," Darby replied. He winked at Jim Plankton. "Put the ad back in your paper."

"I'll do it, Mr. Buckingham," the editor replied, "right along with the entire story so far."

"Just be sure and state how I demanded to search the headquarters," Salton groused.

Darby shook his head with disgust. The sheriff hadn't demanded anything. And if there was a way to solve all this, it was to lure Paxton away long enough to rescue Magdalena. She'd tell the truth to everyone and Paxton would swing for murder. That was why they were going mustanging one more time.

CHAPTER 13

Jory Parnes hadn't said much on the ride back to town and Darby knew he was angry. When they reached the livery and said good-by to Plankton and the sheriff, Darby decided it was time to explain his plans to the young man. From the expression on Jory's face, Darby had a feeling his friend was planning to ride back that night and rescue the girl. It was just the kind of thing Paxton would be expecting and Darby told him so.

"Jory, don't worry, she's all right and, if we use our brains instead of acting rashly, we'll have her back safely."

Jory nodded wearily. "All right. You say the thing to do is to hire another crew and go back out there like we wanted to catch mustangs. Then Paxton is bound to come huntin' our hides. When he does, we somehow give him the slip and outrun him back to the ranch where we rescue Maggie. Now," Jory said cryptically, "is there anything I've missed? Because I don't think it's going to work."

"Why not?" Darby asked glumly. He knew the plan had its shortcomings. But the way Jory talked, the whole idea sounded ridiculous.

"To begin with, after Jim Plankton writes up what happened the last time we tried, there won't be a man in Nevada who would go with us. Even if you paid a hundred, two hundred dollars a month. People aren't stupid," Jory said doggedly. "They know what's happened and, to tell you the truth, I think Paxton is going to be worse than Hench ever was once he gets the feel of power."

"That's why we've got to stop him," Darby insisted.

"Then why didn't you let me try when I had the chance?" Jory said angrily.

"Because you didn't have a chance," Darby argued. "In case you didn't notice, there were a lot of gunmen standing around. It would have been a pointless slaughter even if you could have outdrawn them and shot Paxton."

"It would have been worth it," Jory said.

"Speak for yourself," Darby grumbled.

"Well, I still don't see how we're going to do it alone."

"We're not," Darby said abruptly. "If it is as you say and no one in Nevada will help, then I suppose I have no choice but to telegraph my friends in Running Springs and ask them to come."

"But we can't wait that long! It might take weeks."

"No, it won't. Unless I'm very mistaken, these friends will be riding hard within an hour. They'll be here in five days. During that time, we can start provisioning ourselves."

Jory didn't look convinced. "How many will be coming?"

"Two."

"Two! Is that all the friends you've got?" he wailed. "We might as well go by ourselves!"

Darby laughed. "You don't know these two men. Bear Timberly and Zack Woolsey are worth any ten of Paxton's crowd. And I mean," he said slowly, "ten apiece."

A knock on his door brought Darby to his feet. "Who is it?" he called.

"Pete Barnum," came a low reply. "I saw your ad for help and I want to talk."

Darby opened the door and saw a man he guessed to be in his late twenties standing in the hallway. He was of average size, but gave the immediate impression of wiry strength and immense vitality.

"I have a proposition for you, Mr. Buckingham."

Darby waved him in, offered him a brandy, which was refused, and sat down in a chair while the stranger began pacing back and forth and talking rapidly. Darby found himself more fascinated by the restless energy of the man than the initial words of his story. He had been born in South Dakota and had even attended college, with the idea of following in his father's footsteps as a schoolteacher. But horses had always been his passion and he'd come to Nevada a year ago attracted by the excitement of chasing mustangs. Since that time, he'd worked for an outfit in the central part of the state.

"But they're doing it all wrong!" he exclaimed.

Darby leaned forward intently. In the past five minutes, he'd realized that Pete Barnum was a bright and intense man who knew what he was talking about. "What do you mean?" he asked.

Barnum spun around. "The methods of catching them, of course. Take the way they're melting mustangs with relay riders. You start out after a herd, and in a few miles, the slowest and weakest will start falling out. Old mares, little colts, weak and defective horses are the first to quit. But you keep them running and every mile or so a few more give up or fall dead." Pete took a deep breath. "You see, since the best are the last to quit, every rider lets the others go until, finally, what started out as a herd of twenty ends up as maybe three or four. And you've likely ruined or wind-broke seven or eight horses in the process!"

"What about the corral?" Darby asked.

"Well . . ." Pete Barnum hesitated, then switched the subject, "first, I want to know a couple of things about you. Then we'll get back to talking about catch corrals."

"Very well, ask away," Darby said evenly.

"I'm here because of the newspaper. I was over to the west, near Battle Mountain, when I read the story. It seems as if you've been raising quite a stir in this country."

Darby shrugged. "I'm glad the word is getting around. I suppose, then, you know why I'm here and what I intend to do."

"If the article was right," Pete said, "you're looking for two things; first, to break one man's rule over all this country and second, to see that mustangs are treated more humanely."

"Correct on both counts."

"Good!" The cowboy smiled. "I don't give a hoot about the first part, but I sure do think I've got an idea that will help you with the second."

"So, you've got an improvement," Darby said, "and it has to do with the corrals. Go on."

Pete's eyes grew bright and eager. He leaned forward a little and scrutinized Darby intently. After a few seconds, he slapped his leg and said, "All right! I take you at your word. Now, here's my idea about how we're going to revolutionize this business overnight and do a favor for those mustangs at the same time."

As he listened, Darby grew more and more convinced that Pete Barnum was on to something that *would* be revolutionary. He claimed the concept was an inspiration, but Darby thought it was probably founded on the basis of a keen intellect and a lifelong study of horses. The idea was so simple that Darby marveled that someone hadn't hit upon it earlier. Yet, great inventions are often great because of their simplicity.

Basically, Pete's idea was founded on the observation that horses will not charge a wall that they can neither see through nor over. In the typical catch corral, such as Darby had just helped to construct, the fence is made of poles. With that type of setup, a mustang, Pete contended, sees daylight and charges blindly toward freedom—often killing or crippling itself in the process.

Why not, Pete asked, devise a technique using poles that could be easily transported by horse and accompanying rolls of light, easy to manipulate canvas? The materials could be precut to form walls that could be erected in a matter of hours rather than the days or weeks it usually took to build a normal corral. And the structure needn't be very sturdy because a mustang would no more attack the canvas than it would the base of a cliff.

"Don't you see!" he cried, "up to now, whole sections of range have been ruled off because of a lack of timber or a canyon. But, with my idea, we could transport everything on a few mules, arrive in the night, set up, and be ready for the chase at dawn. It makes me shudder to think of all the months I've worked, trying to build pole corrals only to have a stray band spot me and then avoid that corral until dooms-day . . . or worse, charge in and break through the far side."

"Magnificent idea!" Darby breathed.

"Sure it is," Pete said enthusiastically, "no more crippled or impaled mustangs that try to bust through the fences. No more twenty-mile relay chases until the best of them drop. This is quick, simple, and humane."

Darby poured another brandy, feeling a growing excite-ment inside as he examined the idea from all angles. It sounded foolproof, yet he wasn't really qualified to judge the behavior of mustangs except when lassoed from a tree or caught in a foot trap. But there was one man he knew who could say for certain whether Pete Barnum's idea was sound or not—Jory Parnes.

Fifteen minutes later, they were in Jory's room and Pete was explaining his idea all over again. And Darby didn't have to ask for Jory's opinion. He saw the same excitement building in his young friend that he'd felt himself.

"It can't miss," Jory declared. "He's done it!"

Darby stoked up a cigar and listened to the two young mustangers discuss refinements. They agreed that the ideal canvas corral would be shaped in a figure eight. That way, several bands could be caught and held during a single drive. Also, they could turn some of their own saddle horses into a captured mustang herd to calm the wilder ones.

"But it will take money," Pete said, "and I'll be honest with you, Mr. Buckingham. If I'd had enough to buy all the canvas we'll need, I'd have done it myself. But I earn mus-tanger's wages and the banks would look kinda unfavorably on a loan to a cowboy with a wild idea. They don't know horses."

"Their lack of understanding is to my benefit then," Darby said quickly. "You figure out how much canvas is needed and I'll see it's found at once, even if I have to hire a wagon to race over to Salt Lake City."

"Oh, you won't have to do that. Between this town and Battle Mountain, I've already got enough located to start piecing it together."

"How much do you need?" Jory asked.

"It's got to be the widest and heaviest canvas to be found. We'll sew it into walls seven feet high and make it long enough so that, when it's unrolled, it will form a couple of corrals a hundred feet in diameter."

"That ought to do it pretty good, all right." Jory nodded. "What about wings?"

"We can use a khakilike cloth that sells very cheaply. Just before I càme over here, I stopped by the general store. He's got rolls of stuff that will do fine. As you know, Jory, mustangs are so spooky you can usually just make furrows in the ground and they won't cross over them."

"That's right. Most anything will do."

"There's one thing we haven't talked about," Darby said evenly. "I've got trouble here and you could get hurt if . . ."

Pete waved him into silence. "Like I said earlier, I know the score. But this is the best mustang country in America. I'm going to make a lot of money before it's over and I'll have fun doing it. So, if you can stop that Hightower crowd from keeping me off this range, I'll be indebted. As far as a crew is concerned, don't worry. I already have a couple of vaqueros and some Indians who have been mustanging longer than any of us. They're the best, and I want the best so this will work for all of us. You just take care of the money and Hightower's people. Leave the mustanging to me, and we'll do fine, Mr. Buckingham."

Darby laughed. "This time, when Paxton Bullock comes

looking for an ambush, he's going to be in for a big surprise. Isn't that right, Jory?"

"You bet!"

Darby walked over to the mustanger and stuck out his hand. "Mr. Barnum, I promise no harm will come to you or your crew. And, if everything goes as you and Jory believe, my only request for providing you with canvas is that you and Jory form a partnership. You have the same ideals and I am a sound enough judge of character to say you'd carve a piece of history together. What do you say?"

Pete Barnum studied them both, then nodded. "I reckon we've got ourselves a partnership," he said huskily. "I've been hoping for something like this to come along for quite some time. Let's go mustanging!"

Darby, Pete, and Jory were on the floor with a sea of canvas stretched all over the room. Each man had a heavy needle and a spool of strong cord and was sewing up a storm when the door crashed in. Darby's first thought was that they'd been caught holding the bag by Paxton Bullock, without a chance at reaching their guns. But he was wrong.

Bear Timberly, shoulder lowered and carrying a shattered door, crashed into the room yelling like some kind of wild animal. Zack Woolsey, a bottle of whiskey in one hand and his big hunting rifle in the other, came roaring in close behind. Both tripped on the canvas and pitched headlong into the room, laughing and whooping.

Darby barely managed to roll sideways to avoid the onslaught. He was in a half crouch when Dolly Beavers hit him. Then, before he could holler, she shrieked with happiness into his ear, so loudly it numbed his hearing.

"Oh, Derby! Derby!" She was all over him. Same perfume that was strong enough to kill insects, same crushing weight and powerful, bear-hugging arms, same full and pressing lips—yes, it was the same old Dolly and he loved it.

"What the hell is goin' on?" Bear roared. He jabbed Zack

hard enough to double him over. "We busted us in on a damn sewin' bee!"

Zack straightened with some difficulty, then swung a well-aimed kick at his big friend that clipped him at the knee and brought him to the floor. "Good Lord!" he exclaimed, "when's the sailin' ship floatin' into Elko?"

"Oh, shut up," Darby strangled, trying to thrash his way out from under Dolly and the canvas. "Dolly, let me up!"

When he finally got untangled, one look at Jory and Pete told him they were both amused and a little overwhelmed.

"These are your friends?" Jory asked with a weak smile.

"Shore, we are," Bear said, heaving himself to his feet and extending a hand.

Jory shook and was almost yanked off his feet.

"Wanna slug?" Zack asked, shoving the bottle at them.

"They don't drink," Darby said.

A look of disbelief swept over the two mountain men. It was replaced by pity.

"Don't matter," Zack muttered, trying to pass it off. He turned to Darby. "If you can stop kissin' long enough, why don't you tell us who we got to shoot so we can get it done and have a party."

"That beard sure is going to tickle," Dolly giggled, playfully yanking on it.

Darby struggled to his feet. He was the last man in the world who wanted to spoil anyone's fun, but the whole thing was getting out of hand. "All right!" he yelled. "Let's get serious."

That startled them. No one had ever heard Darby yell before. Before the shock wore off, he said, "Bear, shove the door back in place and then let's all settle down. What we're facing is the most powerful crew in Nevada—not just a man. Didn't you read the telegram?"

"We can't read," Zack said in a truculent voice, "you know that."

He turned to Dolly. She could read.

Dolly shrugged. "We were so happy to get out of our

hotel business, we didn't go beyond the part about you wanting us. You still need us, don't you?" she asked petulantly.

Blast! Now he felt guilty and unreasonable. After all, they
had raced to his aid over more than two hundred miles.

"I'm sorry but what we're up against is more than you
know and the stakes are high." He took the bottle from
Zack. "Let's have a drink and I'll tell you the whole story.
Then maybe you'll see why this isn't the time for a party."

Bear and Zack glanced at each other. Their expressions
were serious but definitely eager. And Darby thought that,
when it came to fighting, they were all business. It was a
good thing too, considering what lay ahead.

CHAPTER 14

They made quite a caravan, Darby thought, as they rode through the middle of town. Besides Zack, Bear, and Jory, there were Pete Barnum and his crew of four mustangers. Darby had insisted that Dolly Beavers remain in Elko, even to the point of threatening to tie her up. In the end, she'd agreed but the farewell had been tearful.

Now, Dolly, as well as most of the town, was out to see them off and there seemed to be a sharp air of expectancy in their leaving. Darby waved to John Salton, who nodded from the doorway of his sheriff's office. Little children trotted along beside until they reached the prairie, and the assortment of accompanying dogs made quite a racket.

It was Darby's intention that their departure should receive as much attention as possible. Mustangs weren't the only animals he intended trapping. That was the reason he'd made sure the editor knew exactly what they were going to do. And, for the past day, all of them had been inundated by questions from the townsfolk about the use of canvas corrals.

Most people seemed to think it was a crazy idea that would never work. In fact, one opportunistic resident was taking bets, three to one, that the mustangs would run right through the flimsy canvas without even missing a stride. Darby matched twenty dollars of that money and Dolly Beavers did the same.

There was another bet that Darby would have taken, and it was that Paxton Bullock would hear the whole story within twenty-four hours. And he'd come riding to stop them. He'd have to. Because Paxton was smart, smart enough to know that his new position of power rested on his ability to keep a stranglehold on Elko's range the way that Hench had done for so many years. And, just as certainly, Paxton was smart enough to realize that Pete Barnum's idea would probably work. If it did, others would follow and soon Paxton's holdings would be halved, then quartered, and halved again. He had to come! The question was—when?

He might wait only until the first roundup. But more likely, Darby thought, Paxton would hit them later, when their guard began to slip. A week. Two weeks. A month. But sometime before they returned in triumph with a herd of captured mustangs.

They spent a morning at the base of the Independence Mountains, cutting cottonwood poles, enough for the double corral Pete envisioned that would form a figure eight. According to Pete's reckoning, they needed seventeen poles, at least ten feet long, for each corral.

The canvas would be unrolled and stretched on the outside of the poles, which Pete wanted to lean slightly toward the center. Then they would guy them with ropes and stakes and pull everything up tight. The wings would veer off from the corral opening at forty-five-degree angles and would require only four-foot poles. When they finished cutting, the mules were loaded and they continued toward the rugged Tuscaroras. On the fifth day, they made their final camp.

"This is it," Jory said, sweeping an arm toward the deep, undulating ridges. "This country is horse heaven and, until now, it's been off limits to mustangers because there's no timber for corrals."

Pete Barnum agreed. "We'll sweep them down into this valley and have men waiting to turn them toward the trap." His eyes shone with intense expectation. "I know it's going to work."

"How soon?" Darby asked.

"Two days ought to do it for the corrals and wings. Another day scouting for herds."

Three days. It seemed unbelievable to Darby that they would be ready that soon. By now, Paxton would be alerted, perhaps calling in his riders from other parts of the range. Darby had questioned Jory closely about that. He'd discovered that there were nearly eighty men on the payroll, but most were scattered over a hundred square miles. Besides, Paxton couldn't pull all of his forces away from his cattle operation. If he wanted to act quickly, he'd summon all the crews that were near headquarters. That meant perhaps twenty, maybe twenty-five, riders. Darby was counting on Paxton moving fast. Everything depended on it. For, if the man brought any more guns for support, no matter what Darby planned, they'd be overrun and wiped out. Pete Barnum and his riders would fight, but they were mustangers, not gunfighters. Any way he cut it, Darby knew they faced long odds.

Paxton Bullock made sure that the girl's door was locked and then he turned back toward the dusty rider. "Tell me the whole story again," he said tightly.

Five minutes later, he dismissed the cowboy and summoned Hart and Tyson out to the veranda. It was cool, and a fresh breeze blew fair and sweet from the mountains, but Paxton was in no mood to enjoy anything. To begin with, Maggie Lamesa had actually bitten him when he tried to kiss her a few hours earlier. He could feel the torn place inside his lip and it hurt almost as much as his pride.

Damn that woman! He'd tried to be a gentleman, though it seemed saving her life should be enough. Deep down, he suspected that she was in love with young Jory Parnes and that was salt in the wound. How could any woman choose Jory over himself? But he had to face it, and it made his stomach twist inside.

A slow smile creased his lips because he knew the solution —kill Jory. That way, she'd stop wishing for him and face the facts of life. And he was tired of coddling her. What that woman needed was a good whipping and more. Paxton figured he'd do it just as soon as he finished with Buckingham and his friends.

Their idea of using canvas intrigued him. It might work. So he'd decided to let them test it out before he attacked. Then he could have the whole setup ready to use and any mustangs they might capture would be an added benefit. Yeah, he liked that.

Paxton turned on the two gunmen and measured their worth so intently they began to squirm. "Buckingham and Jory Parnes have teamed up with an outsider," he said. "They're using some kind of new-fangled idea for catching horses with a canvas corral."

"Hell," Tyson said with derision, "a canvas corral! That's crazy."

"Maybe, maybe not," Paxton replied, "but, just out of curiosity, I'd like to see what happens. I want you both to watch. Don't do anything until you see what they do, then one of you come back and report to me."

Bud Hart grimaced. "But . . . but you know it ain't going to work. Why don't we just get the job done once and for all? If you're worried about what the girl will think, I . . ."

Paxton took one step forward and slapped him square in the face. Hart reeled back, struck the porch railing and, instinctively, his hand dropped toward his gun. But Paxton anticipated him and pulled iron first. Hart's body stiffened, his eyes grew wide with fear as he stared down the barrel.

"Don't think, Hart," Paxton whispered, "just do what I tell you and live. Understand?"

Hart nodded vigorously.

"Good." Paxton reholstered his gun feeling better than he had a few minutes ago. If there'd been any doubt in their minds about his skill, it was gone now. "Get your gear and ride. I'll expect to hear something within three or four days."

He started to walk away, but turned back. "Whatever you

do, don't let them spot you. It's my guess they'll be expecting trouble and be on the lookout."

Tyson cocked his stetson back and peered toward the eastern mountains. "How many riders do they have?" he asked softly.

"Nine." Paxton smiled. "We'll hit them with more than twenty. This time, there won't be any mistakes. I've heard it said that Darby Buckingham is a writer. The only thing left for him to write now is his obituary."

After they'd gone, Paxton sauntered back into the ranch house. He strode over to Maggie Lamesa's door, started to knock, then decided the hell with it. This was his house. He could come and go as he damn well pleased. So, without warning, he threw the door open.

"What do you want?" she demanded. She was standing in the corner of the room, a hairbrush in her hand.

He stood in the doorway, feeling waves of anger and humiliation. He could understand the anger. But why humiliation and even confusion when he faced this girl? Though she was probably ten years younger, it was at times like this that she made him feel like a truant schoolboy.

He gazed at her, feeling the heat rise in his cheeks. "Magdalena . . ."

"Maggie," she spat.

"All right," he said contritely, "how's the shoulder feeling?"

She glared at him.

"Your, ah . . . your face. There's no scabs anymore. You look real nice with your hair combed and all. Would you like to sit on the veranda awhile? We could talk."

"Talk! About what? How you killed my father and Jerome Jerome?"

Even before he realized what he was doing, the gun was in his fist, shaking like a finger of death. If she had cried out, stepped back in fear, even blinked, he'd have pulled the trigger. But she did none of those things. She didn't even shift those penetrating, accusing eyes from his own.

"I ought to kill you, Magdalena," he rasped.

"I'd rather you did than . . . ," she couldn't say it.

The gun sagged in his hand and he leaned up against the doorway. "Is it Jory Parnes? Huh? Is that what it is?"

She turned her back on him. "Go away," she said.

When he couldn't see her face, she had no power over him. In two bounds, he had her by the shoulder and spun her around. He shut his eyes to block out her face and his lips sought hers. When her teeth drew blood, he reared back and struck her. Then she was on the floor, her hair spilled outward to hide that terrible, hating, mocking expression that made him powerless.

"You're going to be mine," he said passionately. "I saved your life and I'll never let you forget that!"

He listened to her low hurt sound for a long time before exiting. Paxton tasted fresh blood in his mouth and, when he slammed the door, he didn't feel the least bit humiliated.

Darby Buckingham woke to a rough shaking. "It's Bear," the voice said. "We got company."

He was instantly awake and sitting up, staring at the massive form that crouched beside him.

"How many?"

"Two."

Darby shook his head. "Only two?"

"Yeah. They snuck in just after sundown. Zack's watching them."

"What are they doing?"

"Making a dry camp," Bear said. "Getting ready to climb into their bedrolls and sleep when I saw 'em last. You want us to bring back their gizzards?"

"No!"

"Why not, damn it?" Bear hissed. "That'd be two less we have to worry about."

Darby slipped out of his blankets and motioned Bear out of earshot of the others. There was no sense in waking everyone up. The news could hold until morning. Besides, tomorrow was set for their test of the canvas corral and he wanted them fresh.

The buffalo hunter was clearly disappointed. "I don't understand why we can't stick 'em and wait for the others," he said roughly, "they'd do it to any of us."

"Suppose they're just a couple of cowboys riding by looking for work?" Darby asked.

"Well, in that case, they're hoss thieves. Both are astraddle Hightower mares. We checked the brands."

"Hmmm," Darby mused, "that means Paxton sent them to spy and report back."

"Hell-fire then! We oughta start carvin'."

"Uh-uh," Darby tried to explain. "If we watch those two, we'll know exactly when Paxton is coming and from where."

Bear scowled, but remained silent.

"The point is," Darby insisted, "as long as you and Zack have them under surveillance, we'll catch mustangs without any worry of attack. Because I know that there isn't a man alive who, on the darkest night, could sneak past you or Zack."

"Well," Bear said, with a deprecating tone in his voice, "that's a mighty nice thing to say."

Darby knew he had his man. Bear and Zack were like children in that they both loved compliments. If given anything approaching an order, they got stubborn and refused on principle. But tell them they were the best and they'd go the limit. Besides, what he said was no more than true. They were hunters and trappers who'd thrived outdoors and faced survival every day of their lives. They could live off the land and melt into their surroundings like Indians. When Paxton came, they'd be waiting with their long buffalo rifles. They wouldn't be seen until the first shot sounded and two horses galloped away with empty saddles.

"You folks ready to catch mustangs tomorrow?"

"I think so," Darby replied. He looked down the hillside toward their corral. The canvas was just light-colored enough to leave a faint impression. "I surely hope this works."

"I bet you do," Bear said. "All that canvas and our supplies must have been enough to outfit a pair of trappers for a whole winter."

"Do you and Zack miss it?"

"Trapping?"

Darby nodded.

"Yeah, sometimes," Bear said quietly. "Running Springs seems mighty congested. Hell, we got three new people just last month! Must be over a hunnert of us altogether."

"That's good for your hotel and saloon business," Darby ventured.

"I wish that business wasn't so good sometimes. Why, when Zack and I closed up to come down here and help you, some of them folks that we threw out of our hotel got real uppity. Can you believe that?"

Darby suppressed a comment. He surely didn't want to get into an argument with Bear, but he didn't quite agree. He decided the best thing to do was divert the conversation. "Did Dolly have rooms for them?"

"I guess so," Bear shrugged. "She found someone to run her place so she could come along."

A wolfish grin crossed Bear's face. "Both Zack and me asked her to marry. I thought you should know we haven't given up on her yet. Maybe we never will."

Darby chose his words carefully. "Dolly is a strong-willed lady."

"Strong-willed! She's crazy for waitin' around for you when she's got Zack and me to choose from."

"Don't shout," Darby hissed, "you're going to wake up the entire camp."

Bear glared at him. "If you hadn't helped us and I didn't like you, I reckon I'd tear down your meathouse right here and now!"

"You've tried before," Darby said, his voice edged with anger. "It didn't work then and it wouldn't work now."

"Are you saying you didn't beat me with a sneak punch?" Bear stepped back, his shoulders bunched aggressively.

Blast! Darby thought. He's ready to fight. The whole thing was absurd. "Maybe I did catch you by surprise," he said. "In fact, I believe I caught you with about six sneak punches."

Bear's shoulders dropped and a low chuckle sounded in his throat. "That's about how many I remember. Glad you fessed up." He hesitated. "The only thing else I want to hear is what your plans are for Dolly."

"To tell you the truth, my friend, I haven't any."

"You what!"

"I haven't any," Darby repeated. "Maybe after this showdown with Paxton Bullock is over, I will. But what we're doing out here and what will happen when Paxton comes is enough to worry about for the time being."

"If you got killed then Dolly would marry me," Bear stated.

"Is that what you want?"

A pained expression crossed Bear's face. "Hell no! What do you think we raced down here for? Sure we like Dolly and think you're loco for not hitchin' up with her. But we'd both fight and die to help a friend. Even if he is a fool."

Darby shook his head in amazement. There wasn't a man living who could have called him a fool and stayed erect except Bear Timberly. But, there weren't many men who'd fight to the death to help him because he was their friend, either.

"Maybe I am what you say, Bear. Yet only a pair like you and Zack are fools enough to save a fool. See what I'm getting at?"

Bear shook his head. "You lost me, but I'll think about it later."

"Good night, friend. Tomorrow we're going to see a new way of catching horses that will change mustanging for the better."

"We'll be watching," Bear said, "and waiting until the

real action starts. Then it'll be our turn to put on the show."

Darby left him and walked back to his bedroll. He had a feeling he wouldn't be able to sleep much. Bear and Zack were a match for anyone, but they used single-shot buffalo rifles. That meant they could stand off a charge of four, perhaps even six, riders. But Paxton wouldn't be leading the charge, and Darby had a feeling there was going to be a whole lot more than six men at his side when he arrived. If Paxton Bullock came with more than a dozen, it was going to be a close, hard fight. And one thing was certain, Darby wasn't about to let Bear and Zack take the brunt of the attack up front and alone.

The friendship went both ways.

CHAPTER 15

He saw them coming, rising up from the brown and gray hills, first no more than tiny specks, then looming bigger against the land. Mustangs! Thirty, at least, by Darby's count. His heart quickened and he watched them intently. Several times, they tried to break out of the path that beckoned them toward the canvas corral. Each time, a rider managed to turn them back. The men rode low, seeming to urge forth every last bit of speed that their horses could give and then ask for more. At first, he'd been able to count three horsemen chasing the mustangs, but at every possible avenue of escape, at the very moment when the wild horses seemed to know they must veer, a rider would suddenly spring from the land and force them onward.

Magnificent riding! Darby recognized a vaquero by the name of Manuel Escobar come racing down a hillside as the stallion made a final bid for freedom. In the clear, high-desert air, he heard Escobar yell and, spurring furiously, the man almost struck the leader, forcing him back.

Did they see the wings yet? Darby's hands clenched and unclenched. For the first time in his life, he wished he too were a horseman. From his hillside vantage point he could almost taste the excitement and drama below.

The riders were fearless. They rode without the thought of what might happen if their horses should trip or step in a hole. Each one seemed to know exactly where he should be and what all the others were doing. They were executing a pincers movement as deftly as a well-trained army. No signal or communication was possible, yet every rider knew that success was based on teamwork.

They seemed to glide over the earth and Darby took a sharp breath as the last rider charged out from his hiding place to make the final push.

Jory Parnes came racing along a hillside so covered with brush that his horse was literally bounding as he spurred in from the side. And, just ahead, the low, stretching wings of their corral were etched on the prairie, like thin, pale arms held open and bidding an embrace.

At the very last moment, the leader tried once more to turn his herd, but Pete Barnum was on him, rope swinging in hand and driving hard. The stallion had no choice but to twist away and race into those wings.

Darby held his breath as they flew into the corral. From his vantage point, he saw the stallion skid to a halt before the canvas he faced, then pivot and race clockwise, searching for an opening that could not be found because Pete Barnum had dismounted on the run and pulled the gate shut.

The stallion kicked the canvas. It held. He drove his mares with teeth into a milling circle. Dust filled the corral and spilled over the sides as Pete's riders formed a protective ring and waited. Five minutes, then ten, and the dust began to settle at last. At a signal from Pete, Escobar peeled back the second gate and the mustangs stampeded into the inner, adjoining corral. Again they circled, kicked at the walls, but finally grouped around the stallion.

Had the corral been made of poles, perhaps the leader would have charged or tried to vault over the top. Maybe he would have been successful but, more likely, he'd have impaled himself on splintered wood or at least broken a leg. But the canvas must have seemed as impregnable to the stallion as if it were the rocky side of a box canyon.

It was over.

Darby laughed out loud and withdrew one of his last Cuban cigars. They'd done it! Pete Barnum's idea would result in the capture of more of these mustangs, but in a humane way. And wild horses that had been shot by cattlemen when their numbers became unmanageable would now be corralled and saddle-broken. The West depended on horses as much as on cattle, good soil, and clear water. Darby knew personally that the U. S. Army was desperate for mounts, and on the prairie, farm animals were badly needed to break the soil and carry families across lonely distances to churches and barn raisings.

And as Darby watched the riders below gather and shake hands, his eyes drifted back to the stallion and his herd. This time, and for a while, man had outsmarted his quarry. But it seemed entirely possible that the mustangs might grow smarter, faster, and stronger in future generations, until the canvas corrals no longer would be so effective. If that happened, the herds would multiply until someone like Pete Barnum devised an even better way to trap them. That might well happen, but the very best wild horses would always remain free.

Darby walked down the hillside toward the waiting men below. He saw Jory, looking a little top-heavy, because the doctor had wrapped his chest and taped it for support. But the young man wasn't feeling any pain now. He came to meet Darby, laughter bubbling in his voice.

"Did you see that!" he exclaimed. "It worked just like Pete Barnum said. Not one horse crippled. And there's some fine animals in there that I can hardly wait to break."

"You'd better let Pete and his men take that part of the job until you're back in shape," Darby said. "I'm sure this is only the beginning."

Darby sauntered over to Barnum and offered his hand. "Pete, you have my congratulations."

Thumbing back his stetson, the mustanger grinned. "Thanks for giving me the chance. This country is alive with mustangs. Some of these we captured are pretty thin because the range is overgrazed."

"What's next?" Darby asked, glancing toward the corral.

"We'll let them settle a few hours before we start to work, taming 'em down. In a couple of days, when they're gentled, we'll go after some more." Pete laughed. "We're in business to stay."

Darby nodded, but remained quiet. He hadn't told them about Bear's visit and the fact that two of Paxton Bullock's men watched at this very moment. He decided to wait until evening. No sense putting a damper on the spirits of everyone until it became necessary.

Just after dark, Bear Timberly slipped into camp and his news made them all forget about mustanging. One of Paxton's stake-out men had just ridden toward the Hightower Ranch. Zack was keeping an eye on the remaining cowboy who didn't seem intent on doing anything. What should they do?

Darby looked pensively at the hillside, beyond where Zack and Paxton's man would be. "What's his camp like, Bear?" he asked, in an almost casual voice.

"A good camp. Hard to spot because it's in a gulley with heavy chaparral."

Darby nodded. "We have to find out what Paxton has in store for us," he told them. "Specifically, we need to know when he's arriving and with how many riders."

Bear shrugged. "If you think the fellar up there knows, Zack and I can try and take him alive."

"Trying isn't good enough." Darby turned to Jory Parnes. "You, Bear, and I are going for a ride," he said. "Let's get saddled."

Bear, Zack, and Jory were in position. They had to be by now, Darby thought, crawling forward, trying to keep himself from becoming tangled in the thick brush. High above, there was a pale three-quarter moon that gave a cold yellow light. He judged it to be about ten o'clock and all the stars were just about in full shine. He rammed into some kind of thorny bush that scratched his face and he choked back an oath. He'd written scenes about Indians and mountain men sneaking up on camps, but none of them had ever plowed into a pile of thorns. He'd crawled only a few hundred yards and his knees hurt from the rocks. Maybe he should have let Zack and Bear do this. But he hadn't, because everything depended on taking Paxton's spy alive. That meant additional risks that Darby was unwilling to share.

He circled the thorn bush and continued forward. Time was running out. Already, the other man would be ten miles away and every second they delayed would give Darby that much less time for preparing a defense.

Suddenly, he heard the nickering of a horse. Darby froze. A branch cracked and he flattened. For a moment, he lay still, almost afraid to breathe. Then, he pulled himself ahead, inch by inch, until he was at the crest of a low rise beyond which was the gulley camp. He carefully pushed some sagebrush aside and his eyes strained to penetrate the blackness. He saw the man! Not forty feet away. All hope that his quarry might be asleep or off-guard vanished. The sound of boots crunched lightly on the dry gulley floor and Darby sensed rather than saw that the man below was alert to danger.

Just then, a rock crashed into brush on the opposite side of the gulley. Instantly, the man whirled and Darby saw his gun belch flame. The sound rolled down the gulley and melted into the distance.

"Hoo-ey!" came Zack's voice, thirty yards up the draw. Again a shot slammed into the night and Darby saw the man below hit the ground.

Silence ensued. Darby peered down at his man and began inching forward.

"Yee-haw!" Jory yelled.

His voice was drowned by two more shots and Paxton's rider scrambled sideways. Darby crabbed ten feet in a rush before the echoes of the gunfire raced out the gulley and vanished.

He has only two bullets left, Darby thought. Then I'll have him in my grasp. He tried to imagine what the cowboy was thinking. Was he thinking at all? By now, he would be aware that he was surrounded. The fact that no one had returned his fire might cause even more fear.

"Ya!" Bear again. A little closer.

Darby rose to crawl when the gunshot would drown out the sound of his movement. But, this time, there was no spitting orange flame. Instead, he heard the pounding of boots and knew what was happening. The man was trying to escape.

There wasn't time for thought or caution. Darby jerked erect and started running toward the sound of the nickering horse he'd heard only moments before.

Hoofs clattered just ahead.

"Hold still, damn it!" came a desperate whisper.

Then, Darby saw him. The cowboy swinging into his saddle, yanking the horse around. He had to come down the gulley. All the sounds he'd heard were off the ridges. He wouldn't go that way. Darby took three strides up the bank of the gulley, and as the horse and rider leapt forward into a run, Darby jumped.

Even though his legs were short and he never did claim great physical agility, he should have struck the rider and toppled him, because the man had to pass just below. But as he pushed off in his leap from the bank, he felt the gravel slide under his feet and knew he wasn't going to make it. Instead of catching the rider up around the shoulders, he struck the horse, knocking it off stride into the bank. The animal lost its footing and crashed over with its legs flailing.

The rider kicked free and Darby rolled. In the half light, everything seemed to move faster. Before Darby was able to come to his feet, the cowboy was leaping into the saddle even as his mount was still scrabbling to right itself. He was a horseman. But he'd gone far enough. Darby made no mistake this time. While the man's total concentration was fixed on getting out, Darby launched himself into a diving tackle before the animal came up on all fours.

A shot exploded almost in his face. Then, Darby's fist did its own exploding. He punched the cowboy twice and yanked the gun loose from his fingers and hurled it away. He then rolled the cowboy over and pulled his wrist up near the shoulder blades.

"Ahhh!"

Darby eased the pressure by lowering the wrist a fraction of an inch. There was no resistance in the man. None at all.

"I want some answers," he snapped, "about Paxton. How many men are coming and how soon?"

No answer.

Darby's jaw muscles tightened and he knew he would break the cowboy's shoulder if that was necessary. He pushed the wrist almost up to the man's neck again. "Talk or I'll break this one and then the other!"

"All right!"

Darby lowered the arm.

"Twenty men. Should be here in two days." He took a deep and ragged gasp of air. "They'll camp halfway tomorrow night."

"Where?"

"Halfway, gawddamnit! I don't know where."

Darby looked up and found his three friends watching.

Zack knelt beside the rider. He grabbed the man by the hair, twisting his face out of the dirt.

"Ahhh!"

"Shore is a fool for hollerin', ain't he," Bear said, overlooking the scene.

Zack's hunting knife scratched at the man's exposed throat. "You telling the truth?"

Darby heard the blade scrape whiskers.

"Yes! Don't do it. Please. I told you the truth."

The knife returned to Zack's sheath. "I think we can believe that," he said quietly.

Darby swallowed hard. For a moment, he'd been half-afraid Zack might actually use the knife. There'd been something in the way he'd asked his question. "Would you . . ." Darby's sentence trailed into silence.

"Naw," Zack replied. "First I'd have built a fire and warmed his bare feet. They always talk real good, then."

"I imagine so," Darby said dryly. He felt satisfied the way things had gone so far.

"We can set up a trap," Jory said.

"It wouldn't work." Darby climbed to his feet. The rider didn't move. "If they discovered this one missing, Paxton would guess what happened. He'd never fall for any surprises."

"So what, then?" Zack asked.

"We go after them," Darby said. "We strike their camp tomorrow night. That's the last thing he'll expect and it's our only hope."

"Now yore talkin'!" Bear said loudly. "Let's go."

After returning to camp with their prisoner, Darby, Bear, Zack, and Jory saddled and rode within the hour. Except for a few short rests, they traveled in a steady, northeasterly direction toward the ranch. At midday, they stopped and made camp in a low spot on the prairie that left them hidden.

As far as Darby could tell from Jory, it was going to be impossible to predict exactly where or when Paxton would camp. He agreed with Jory that the man would halt for the night. As far as Paxton was concerned, there wasn't any threat and no hurry. And he'd want his force to be well rested and steady.

They decided that they should remain hidden until dark, then travel cautiously until they found Paxton. With luck, they could sneak into their midst and capture the entire bunch without firing a shot.

At least, that's what Darby was hoping as they rode from the low ground just after dark. He didn't even want to think about the slim possibility that they might actually pass their quarry unseen in the dark. If that happened, Pete Barnum and his mustangers would be totally defenseless. By the time Darby discovered such a mistake, they'd be miles behind and helpless to come to the rescue. So, as they rode on, Darby's stomach grew tighter and tighter.

Actually, he would never have attempted finding Paxton at night except for the presence of Zack and Bear. They claimed they could smell a man in the dark and he believed them. They also claimed they could hear hoofbeats for a distance of three miles on hard ground; he believed that, too. But, as the night grew longer, he began to worry more and more. Could they, somehow, have slipped by?

Three hours before dawn, he knew the answer.

The campfire was no more than a bed of dying coals, but Zack and Bear reined their horses to a stop about the same time.

"There?" Zack asked, pointing slightly to the north.

Bear lifted his nose like a wild animal sniffing the wind. A moment passed while Darby leaned forward expectantly in his saddle.

"Yeah," Bear said in a way that left no doubt in Darby's mind, "maybe a little bit east of where you're pointing."

"Far?" Darby asked.

"Hard to say," Zack offered. "We're riding into a breeze. But I'd reckon not more than two miles."

Bear nodded soundlessly, then dismounted with Zack following the example. "We'd better walk from here on," he explained.

"Why?" Darby asked. He wasn't arguing, but it did go against his nature when a horse was available.

"When our animals catch the smell of theirs, then they just might start whinneying. We have to be ready to clamp their muzzles before that happens."

"Oh," Darby replied, "that's why we won't leave them here?"

"Yep," Bear mumbled, "when we're ready to fight, the horses can do what they damn well please. No one would hear them over the sound of gunfire."

Darby stepped in front of Bear, but his words were meant

for all of them. "We're going to give them a chance to sur-
render," he said stubbornly.

"Like they gave Jerome Jerome?" Jory shot back. "If we
fail, what happens to Magdalena?"

"We won't fail," Darby replied tightly, "but this isn't
going to be a slaughter, either." Then, before anyone else
could argue, he started toward Paxton's camp.

He'd closed the distance by half when he saw the firelight
suddenly grow bright. And, dimly, he heard a rough and
rousing voice in the distance. Blast! They were being
awakened.

"That's it," Zack spat, swinging into his saddle.

Darby nodded and wearily mounted. If only they'd
waited just another half hour. Maybe they could have taken
the whole camp by surprise. Maybe there would have been
no bloodshed. But that hope was dashed. Bitter, he yanked
his shotgun out of the scabbard and whipped his horse into
a gallop.

Side by side, they were four men riding at a hard gallop
across the prairie toward a fire that leapt ever brighter
against the black night. Darby's reins were tied together and
he dropped them on the horse's neck and cocked the hammers on both barrels. In the pale moonlight, he glanced
sideways and saw how white and young Jory's expression
appeared. Of the four, Jory mattered the most. He was in
love and too young to die.

Fortunately, the earth over which they raced was grass-
covered and hoofs made almost no sound. Up ahead, Paxton's crew would be half-asleep, half-dressed. If they could
only cover the distance in time, there might still be a
chance.

But someone was rousing them, and the nearer they came,
the more that someone sounded like Paxton Bullock. That
made Darby ride harder than he'd ever ridden in his life.

CHAPTER 16

Paxton didn't yell until it was too late. Just a hundred yards away, Darby saw him loom into the firelight, then begin to kick it furiously into the sky. The sparks ignited the air and Darby's horse shied away, almost spilling him from the saddle. Burning wood flew in all directions, even onto some bedrolls and riders. Yet, the action was effective because the firelight was gone; Darby had the impression of running blindly down a cave.

His horse struck someone. A gun flashed off toward his left. Zack's big buffalo rifle roared in response and the gun flashed again, but this time at the ground.

The air boiled with shots and smoke but Darby held his own fire. Some men, dressed only in longjohns, angled past a burning log, running barefoot in full flight. Darby hoped there were plenty of others with the same idea.

A bullet plucked the buckskin shirt he wore and Darby decided his chances for survival were better on the ground. He yanked hard on the reins and fell from the saddle. Two guns opened up, blinking in the night like cat's eyes. Darby swung the rifle and fired. The eyes went out.

Again the awesome booming of a high caliber rifle. Something moved very close and Darby yanked the shotgun up. Jory! His finger was squeezing but, at the last instant, he jerked it sideways.

Someone cursed and he pivoted around just in time to see a man charge. Darby jumped to his feet and met him strength for strength. Then he stepped back and swung. His attacker flipped over backward and didn't move.

Gunshots. Running hoofbeats. Oaths and a moaning sound. Then—silence. "Jory! Bear! Zack!" he whispered.

A pistol flashed and Darby grabbed his arm in pain as another gun answered three times. Darby heard the sound of snapping brush and a thud. Farther away, hoofbeats receding into the night.

"Darby, are you hurt?" Jory was beside him, his gun still in his fist.

"No," Darby gritted. He tested his fingers and knew the bullet was only flesh deep.

"Where are Zack and Bear?"

"God only knows," Jory breathed, "after they used those big rifles, they were on foot. I damn near shot Bear. Couldn't see well."

"I know," Darby muttered, thinking about how terribly close he'd come to gunning Jory by mistake. "It certainly happened fast. Where did everyone go?"

"Most of them ran, I think. Only about five or six stayed to fight." Jory shook his head. "Man, we did it. We beat them!"

"Paxton," Darby clipped, "did we get Paxton!"

Jory's face jerked toward Darby's. "I . . . I don't know." He placed a hand on Darby's shoulder. When he spoke, his voice was flat and knife-edged. "I can't take the chance he might have escaped. I'm riding."

"We're riding," Darby said. He yanked his sleeve up and strode over to a man's scattered bedroll. Ignoring the pain, he ripped a blanket strip away and wound it about his forearm. "Tie it for me, will you? Then find a couple of horses as quickly as you can."

"What about Zack and Bear?"

"What about us?" Zack asked, stepping out of the night with Bear in tow.

"Damn!" Bear swore, grasping Darby's arm. His thick fingers quickly examined the wound. "It's not bad," he said after a moment. "Deep enough but it didn't touch bone."

"There's some men around here who are hurt much worse," Darby said. "Have either of you seen Paxton?"

"We don't know what he looks like," Zack grunted.

Darby described the man. They hadn't seen anyone like him. Somehow, Darby knew that Paxton must have escaped. Bullock just wasn't the type of man to scatter and run in panic like most of his riders.

"Can you two take care of the wounded and round up the others? Jory and I have to go after Paxton."

"Yeah," Bear said. "But we'd sure rather go with you than play nursemaid to a bunch of sneakin' coyotes."

"I know," Darby said simply. "But as soon as you finish up here, start back to Elko. These men are going to jail and if the sheriff gives you trouble, put him in with them. Then tell Dolly I'm all right."

At the mention of her name, some of the disappointment slipped from their faces.

"Thanks," Darby said. "Now, let's find some horses."

Five minutes later, Darby and Jory were mounted and ready to ride. They would lead two fresh horses and use them for the last stretch. There was still a chance they could overtake Paxton, but every moment delayed sliced the odds. Darby had reloaded his shotgun and shoved it into his saddle boot. Dawn was starting to turn the blackness gray. It was time for a horse race.

They pushed hard, racing into the sunrise, covering ground in a rush. Both men were grim-faced, drawn. Two straight hours they galloped and Darby felt his horse starting to labor. He pushed it another mile and the animal was faltering badly.

"How much farther?" Darby called. His horse tripped in exhaustion and Darby reined to a halt and unloaded. "Mine is finished. I won't run him to death."

"We're getting close," Jory said, peering bleakly into the distance. "Have you been watching them?"

"Who?" Darby hadn't been watching anything. The pain

in his arm throbbed through his whole body and, not being the rider Jory was, every ounce of concentration he could muster was directed at staying in the saddle and making the horse's running as easy as possible.

"Paxton! He and another rider." Jory pointed down at the tracks. "We're not fifteen minutes behind them."

Darby stared at the tracks, followed them with his eyes into the empty distance. "I don't see anyone. Are you sure?"

"Hell, yes! I spotted them on the ridge just after sunrise. Couple more times since."

"Can we overtake them before they reach headquarters?"

Jory bailed out of his saddle and grabbed for his cinch strap. "Let's give it a try," he said. "They've got only two horses; we've got four. It's time to switch. We're ten miles from Maggie, but they're less than eight. It'll be close."

Darby ripped the cinch loose and yanked the saddle off his horse. The animal didn't seem to notice; its head was down and it was blowing hard. Even its face was covered with white foam and sweat. He chose the larger of the two spare horses and dropped the blankets and saddle in place. Jory switched bridles and helped him mount. He needed help. Hard riding seemed to have kept his blood pumping and the bullet wound bleeding. His sleeve was sopping wet and the arm felt numb. As he tottered into the saddle, he somehow lost his balance and almost fell.

Jory's hand steadied him. Without speaking, the young man yanked up Darby's sleeve and unwound the blanket strip. Jory's lips were thin and white. "You can't go on."

"A tourniquet," Darby breathed. "Put one on."

Jory's mouth opened to protest.

"Please," Darby whispered, "I can make ten miles and still be some help. Do it, Jory, for me. For Maggie!"

He nodded and did as asked. Then they were spurring into a gallop. Every few minutes, Darby lifted his eyes, hoping to see Paxton growing closer. Once he did see them, but they seemed a long, long way off.

"We're closing," Jory shouted. "Hold on, you'll make it!"

Darby forced a grin. He followed Jory's pointing arm.
They *were* closing. But would they be in time? And, if so,
could he handle his share of the fight? There was nothing he
could do but hang on and try—he thought he would last that
long before he passed out.

They almost caught Paxton and Tyson. Over the last few
miles, Darby and Jory cut the distance to less than a thousand yards. But, as the ranch grew close, Darby, leaning
heavily on the saddle horn, knew it might as well have been
a thousand miles. Maybe Bear or Zack could have shot the
pair with an extra charge of powder in their buffalo rifles.
But, outside of that, there wasn't a damn thing anyone could
have done to stop Paxton from reaching the headquarters
and Magdalena Lamesa.

The horses they pursued were staggering visibly. Had the
ranch been two miles farther, they wouldn't have made it.
Darby swore in frustration. Paxton's luck was holding.
Somehow, he'd been able to escape, and being a horseman,
he'd calculatingly used his horseflesh to the very limit.

Darby saw Paxton and Tyson tearing into the ranch yard,
dismount at a run, and blast through the front door.

It *had* been a horse race. But they'd lost.

"Whoa-up," he ordered, reining his mount to a standstill.

They halted just outside of rifle range. Everything grew
still and Darby dismounted, surprised to find he still had
strength in his legs. He shook his head, trying to think. They
couldn't just charge the ranch house. They'd be shot out of
their saddles before they traversed the yard. He looked over
at Jory. "You know the layout better than I," he said wearily. "How do we get close enough for me to use a shotgun?"

Jory started to answer, then stiffened. He was looking past
Darby. In a tone as cold as blizzard wind, he said, "We don't
have to. They're coming after us."

Darby followed his gaze, felt a crushing sense of despair
at what he saw. Maggie was being half-dragged, half-

carried by Paxton Bullock. Beside them strode a tall, fluid man with a tied-down gun.

"Why should they take refuge?" Darby sighed. "As far as they're concerned, we're practically harmless. Paxton knows you have cracked ribs and believes you can't draw. I'm hurt and a miserable shot under any circumstances. And they've got Maggie as a shield."

Jory spun the cylinder on his Smith & Wesson. Very carefully, he pushed the barrel in behind his belt. He wet his lips with the tip of his tongue and pulled his hat down low over his eyes. Eyes that burned with intensity. "If I get the chance, my second bullet is for Tyson."

Darby yanked his shotgun out of the rifle boot. He cocked both hammers and crooked it over his bloody sleeve. "The other man. Is he good?"

A cold, cynical smile. "Yeah. Probably faster than Paxton and me both."

Darby knew there was nothing more to be said. He took a deep breath and let it out slowly. It seemed to clear a ringing sound in his ears. He focused unsteadily on the two men and saw they wore almost identical smiles. They were *so* confident.

As soon as Maggie saw Jory and Darby, she stopped fighting. And now, as Darby watched her, he saw hope in her eyes. Maggie's chin was high, and though she looked unusually pale, she preceded Bullock with a dignity and bearing Darby would never have expected from a hard-raised mustanger's daughter.

They stopped at twenty paces. Both of their guns were holstered. Paxton's left hand drew Maggie closer. His right hand didn't stray more than an inch from his gun butt. "Well," he drawled, "I couldn't have asked for anything finer. Buckingham, you're holding a shotgun. You going to use it on me and the girl?" He almost laughed.

"Let her go," Darby said tonelessly.

"Sure," Paxton sneered.

Maggie suddenly twisted and, for an instant, Jory might

have had a clear target. But the chance was gone now and Paxton's arm locked around her neck and drew her to his body. "Be still!"

"Steady, Jory," Darby hissed, never taking his eyes off Paxton's gunfighter.

"Can't you see?" Jory said loudly. "She hates you. It's me she loves. No matter what you do, she'll never change."

"Shut up!" Paxton growled. He eased the pressure around her neck. His next words were for her. "Is . . . is that what you'd settle for? You'd take him over me?" There was pain in his voice. And disbelief.

"Yes!" she choked. "I hate you. I love him!"

A wildness flared in his eyes.

Tyson's head didn't move an inch, but his eyes shifted sideways. "Come on, boss," he said urgently, "enough talk."

"You and me," Jory pleaded, looking at Paxton. "Best man wins her. Or are you a coward?"

"Boss!"

Paxton kept the girl at his side. "I'm going to show her who's the coward," he rasped. "Tyson, when I put a bullet through Jory, Buckingham will have to pick one of us."

"I choose you," Darby said.

"Then you'll kill the girl, too. That shotgun ain't choosey. And if that makes you squirm, know this—my second bullet has *your* name on it."

Darby blinked, felt sweat running through his beard. Paxton had it all figured.

Almost.

Jory Parnes had the right side of Paxton as a target. Eight inches wide, six feet and more. He needed the edge and he took it. The left hand. The hand that had eased up near his belt while Paxton's attention was riveted on the right. The left hand that streaked for the Smith & Wesson traveling no more than three inches. His hand closed on the gun butt even as Paxton seemed to realize he'd been fooled and desperately made his own play.

Jory's six gun was out, and he began firing. Steadily, deliberately, in a stitching pattern up and down that eight inches of flesh. Paxton, gun halfway out of his holster, didn't flinch when the first bullet struck. But his hand spasmed and his gun fell from his grasp.

Darby flipped the shotgun from his forearm. It fell in line with Tyson's body and he jerked both triggers just as the gunfighter began to shoot.

He'd lied to Paxton. Tyson was his target from the very beginning. Tyson, who'd waited one heartbeat too long for Darby to swing his weapon away. Tyson, who never knew what hit him as he lifted from the ground and slammed over backward.

Darby let the shotgun slip out of his hands and fall to the grass. The acrid smell of gun smoke was thick and he saw Jory and the girl embrace in the swirling cloud of it.

Darby Buckingham began to sway toward the ranch house. Inside, maybe he'd be able to find a decent bottle of brandy and a good cigar. Yes, and a soft chair, too. Then he'd sleep. Just sleep and dream about Dolly and wild horses. Good things both. The woman. The mustangs.

AFTERWORD

While the story and main characters are fictional, *Mustang Fever* is based on a good deal of solid historical fact. There was a man called Mustang Grey, who lassoed a wild one from the branch of a tree, and foot traps saved more than one cowboy from a long walk.

Perhaps most interesting was the man named Pete Barnum. He actually did come to Nevada, and revolutionized mustanging with his portable canvas corral. Mr. Barnum became the dominant force in mustanging history. But in later years when the demand for good saddle horses fell and the mustang became more valuable for his meat and hide, Pete Barnum called it quits. He had too much love and respect for mustangs to do otherwise. No one is sure what happened to the man. He vanished from the pages of history, never to be heard from again. But today, in the vast Nevada deserts and mountain ranges, the mustangs are holding their own. I kind of think Pete Barnum would have liked that very much.